Alfred Ainger, Thomas Hood

Poems of Thomas Hood

Volume 1

Alfred Ainger, Thomas Hood

Poems of Thomas Hood
Volume 1

ISBN/EAN: 9783337368562

Printed in Europe, USA, Canada, Australia, Japan

Cover: Foto ©Andreas Hilbeck / pixelio.de

More available books at **www.hansebooks.com**

A LIST OF BOOKS

RECENTLY PUBLISHED BY

EDWARD MOXON, 44, DOVER STREET.

MISCELLANEOUS.

I.

HAYDN'S DICTIONARY OF DATES, and

UNIVERSAL REFERENCE, relating to all Ages and Nations; comprehending every Remarkable Occurrence, Ancient and Modern—the Foundation, Laws, and Governments of Countries —their Progress in Civilisation, Industry, and Science — their Achievements in Arms; the Political and Social Transactions of the British Empire—its Civil, Military, and Religious Institutions—the Origin and Advance of Human Arts and Inventions, with copious details of England, Scotland, and Ireland. The whole comprehending a body of information, Classical, Political, and Domestic, from the earliest accounts to the present time. THIRD EDITION. In one volume, 8vo, price 18s. cloth.

II.

KNOWLES'S (JAMES) PRONOUNCING AND

EXPLANATORY DICTIONARY OF THE ENGLISH LANGUAGE. Founded on a correct development of the Nature, the Number, and the Various Properties of all its Simple and Compound Sounds, as combined into Syllables and Words. A NEW EDITION. In medium 8vo, price 10s. 6d. cloth.

III.

By the AUTHOR OF "TWO YEARS BEFORE THE MAST."

DANA'S SEAMAN'S MANUAL; containing a

Treatise on Practical Seamanship, with Plates; a Dictionary of Sea Terms; Customs and Usages of the Merchant Service; Laws relating to the Practical Duties of Master and Mariners. SECOND EDITION. Price 5s. cloth.

IV.

HINTS ON HORSEMANSHIP, to a NEPHEW
and NIECE; or, Common Sense and Common Errors in Common
Riding. By Colonel GEORGE GREENWOOD, late of the Second
Life Guards. Price 2s. 6d.

V.

CICERO'S LIFE AND LETTERS. The Life
by Dr. MIDDLETON; The Letters translated by WM. MELMOTH
and Dr. HEBERDEN. In one volume, 8vo, with Portrait and
Vignette, price 16s. cloth.

VI.

ELLEN MIDDLETON. A TALE. By LADY
GEORGIANA FULLERTON. SECOND EDITION. In three volumes,
price 31s. 6d. cloth.

VII.

CAPTAIN BASIL HALL'S FRAGMENTS OF
VOYAGES AND TRAVELS. A NEW EDITION. In one volume,
8vo, price 12s. cloth.

VIII.

THE WISDOM AND GENIUS OF THE
RIGHT HON. EDMUND BURKE, illustrated in a series of
Extracts from his Writings and Speeches; with a Summary of
his Life. By PETER BURKE, Esq. Post 8vo, price 10s. 6d. cloth.

IX.

TALFOURD'S (MR. SERJEANT) VACATION
RAMBLES AND THOUGHTS; comprising the Recollections
of three Continental Tours in the Vacations of 1841, 42, and 43.
SECOND EDITION. In one volume, price 10s. 6d. cloth.

X.

DYCE'S REMARKS ON MR. C. KNIGHT'S
AND MR. J. P. COLLIER'S EDITIONS OF SHAKSPEARE. In
8vo, price 9s. cloth.

XI.

LIFE IN THE SICK-ROOM: ESSAYS. By
AN INVALID. SECOND EDITION. Price 8s. boards.

XII.

SHELLEY'S (MRS.) RAMBLES IN GERMANY
AND ITALY in 1840, 1842, and 1843. In 2 vols. post 8vo, price 21s. cloth.

XIII.

PAST AND PRESENT POLICY OF ENG-
LAND TOWARDS IRELAND. SECOND EDITION. Post 8vo, price 9s. cloth.

XIV.

THE LIFE OF LORD CHANCELLOR HARD-
WICKE; with Selections from his Correspondence, Diaries, Speeches, and Judgments. By GEORGE HARRIS, Esq., of the Middle Temple, Barrister-at-Law. *In the Press.*

D'ISRAELI'S WORKS.

I.

CURIOSITIES OF LITERATURE. THIRTEENTH
EDITION. In one volume, 8vo, with Portrait, Vignette, and Index, price 16s. cloth.

II.

MISCELLANIES OF LITERATURE. In one
volume, 8vo, with Vignette, price 14s. cloth.

CONTENTS :—

1. LITERARY MISCELLANIES.
2. QUARRELS OF AUTHORS.
3. CALAMITIES OF AUTHORS.
4. THE LITERARY CHARACTER.
5. CHARACTER OF JAMES THE FIRST.

DYCE'S BEAUMONT AND FLETCHER.

THE WORKS OF BEAUMONT AND
FLETCHER; the Text formed from a new collation of the early Editions. With Notes and a biographical Memoir. By the Rev. A. DYCE. In eleven volumes 8vo. Price 6l. 12s., cloth.

SHELLEY'S WORKS.

I.

SHELLEY'S POETICAL WORKS. Edited by
Mrs. Shelley. In one volume, 8vo, with Portrait and Vignette,
price 10s. 6d. cloth.

II.

SHELLEY'S ESSAYS and LETTERS FROM
ABROAD. Edited by Mrs. Shelley. A New Edition.
Price 5s.

DRAMATIC LIBRARY.

I.

BEAUMONT AND FLETCHER. With an
INTRODUCTION. By George Darley. In two volumes, 8vo,
with Portraits and Vignettes, price 32s. cloth.

II.

SHAKSPEARE. With REMARKS on his LIFE
and WRITINGS. By Thomas Campbell. In one volume,
8vo, with Portrait, Vignette, and Index, price 16s. cloth.

III.

BEN JONSON. With a MEMOIR. By William
Gifford. In one volume, 8vo, with Portrait and Vignette,
price 16s. cloth.

IV.

MASSINGER AND FORD. With an INTRO-
DUCTION. By Hartley Coleridge. In one volume, 8vo, with
Portrait and Vignette, price 16s. cloth.

V.

WYCHERLEY, CONGREVE, VANBRUGH,
AND FARQUHAR. With BIOGRAPHICAL and CRITICAL
NOTICES. By Leigh Hunt. In one volume, 8vo, with Portrait
and Vignette, price 16s. cloth.

VI.

SHERIDAN'S DRAMATIC WORKS. With
a BIOGRAPHICAL and CRITICAL SKETCH. By Leigh
Hunt. Price 5s. 6d. cloth.

ROGERS'S POEMS.

I.

ROGERS'S POEMS. A New Edition. In one
volume, illustrated by 72 Vignettes, from designs by Turner
and Stothard, price 16s. boards.

II.

ROGERS'S ITALY. A New Edition. In one
volume, illustrated by 56 Vignettes, from designs by Turner
and Stothard, price 16s. boards.

III.

ROGERS'S POEMS; AND ITALY. In two
pocket volumes, illustrated by numerous Woodcuts, price 10s.
cloth.

WORDSWORTH'S POEMS.

I.

WORDSWORTH'S POETICAL WORKS. In
six volumes, price 30s. cloth.

II.

WORDSWORTH'S POETICAL WORKS. In
one volume, medium 8vo, price 20s. cloth.

III.

WORDSWORTH'S POEMS, chiefly of early and
late Years, including "The Borderers," a Tragedy. In one
volume, price 9s. cloth.

IV.

WORDSWORTH'S SONNETS. In one Volume,
price 6s. cloth.

V.

WORDSWORTH'S EXCURSION. A Poem.
In one volume, price 6s. cloth.

CAMPBELL'S POEMS.

I.

CAMPBELL'S POETICAL WORKS. A New

Edition. In one volume, illustrated by 20 Vignettes from designs by Turner, and 37 Woodcuts from designs by Harvey. Price 20s. boards.

II.

CAMPBELL'S POETICAL WORKS. In one

pocket volume, illustrated by numerous Woodcuts, price 8s. cloth.

III.

THE LIFE AND LETTERS OF CAMPBELL.

Edited by Dr. William Beattie, one of his Executors.

In the Press.

CHAUCER AND SPENSER.

I.

CHAUCER'S POETICAL WORKS. With an

Essay on his Language and Versification, and an Introductory Discourse; together with Notes and a Glossary. By Thomas Tyrwhitt. In one volume, 8vo, with Portrait and Vignette, price 16s. cloth.

II.

SPENSER'S WORKS. With a Selection of

Notes from various Commentators; and a Glossarial Index: to which is prefixed some account of the Life of Spenser. By the Rev. Henry John Todd, M.A., Archdeacon of Cleveland. In one volume, 8vo., with Portrait and Vignette, price 16s. cloth.

CHARLES LAMB'S WORKS.

I.

LAMB'S WORKS. A New Edition. In one

volume, 8vo, with Portrait and Vignette, price 14s. cloth.

II.

THE ESSAYS OF ELIA. A New Edition.

Price 5s.

POETRY.

TENNYSON'S POEMS.   2 vols.   Price 12s. boards.

MILNES'S POEMS.   4 vols.   Price 20s. boards.

TRENCH'S JUSTIN MARTYR, and other Poems.   6s. bds.

——————— POEMS from Eastern Sources.   Price 6s. bds.

BROWNING'S PARACELSUS.   Price 6s. boards.

——————— SORDELLO.   Price 6s. 6d. boards.

PATMORE'S (COVENTRY) POEMS.   Price 5s. bds.

BARRETT'S (MISS) POEMS.   2 vols.   Price 12s. bds.

HOOD'S POEMS.   2 vols.   Price 12s. boards.

(In 24mo.)

TALFOURD'S (SERJEANT) TRAGEDIES.   Price 2s. 6d.

TAYLOR'S PHILIP VAN ARTEVELDE.   Price 2s. 6d.

——————— EDWIN THE FAIR, &c.   Price 2s. 6d.

BARRY CORNWALL'S SONGS.   Price 2s. 6d.

LEIGH HUNT'S POETICAL WORKS.   Price 2s. 6d.

PERCY'S RELIQUES.   3 vols.   Price 7s. 6d.

LAMB'S DRAMATIC SPECIMENS.   2 vols.   Price 5s.

KEAT'S POETICAL WORKS.   Price 2s. 6d.

SHELLEY'S MINOR POEMS.   Price 2s. 6d.

CHEAP EDITIONS OF POPULAR WORKS.

SHELLEY'S ESSAYS AND LETTERS. Price 5s.

SEDGWICK'S LETTERS FROM ABROAD. Price 2s. 6d.

DANA'S TWO YEARS BEFORE THE MAST. 2s. 6d.

CLEVELAND'S VOYAGES AND COMMERCIAL EN-
TERPRISES. Price 2s. 6d.

ELLIS'S EMBASSY TO CHINA. Price 2s. 6d.

PRINGLE'S RESIDENCE IN SOUTH AFRICA. 3s. 6d.

THE ESSAYS OF ELIA. Price 5s.

HUNT'S INDICATOR, AND COMPANION. Price 5s.

———— THE SEER; OR, COMMON-PLACES RE-
FRESHED. Price 5s.

SHERIDAN'S DRAMATIC WORKS. With an INTRO-
DUCTION. By LEIGH HUNT. Price 5s.

LAMB'S LIFE AND LETTERS. Price 5s.

———— ROSAMUND GRAY, &c. Price 2s. 6d.

———— TALES FROM SHAKSPEARE. Price 2s. 6d.

———— ADVENTURES OF ULYSSES. To WHICH IS
ADDED, MRS. LEICESTER'S SCHOOL. Price 2s.

HALL'S VOYAGE TO LOO-CHOO. Price 2s. 6d.

———— TRAVELS IN SOUTH AMERICA. Price 5s.

CAMPBELL'S POETICAL WORKS. Price 2s. 6d.

LAMB'S POETICAL WORKS. Price 1s. 6d.

BAILLIE'S (JOANNA) FUGITIVE VERSES. Price 1s.

SHAKSPEARE'S POEMS. Price 1s.

Bradbury & Evans, Printers, Whitefriars.

POEMS.

POEMS

BY

THOMAS HOOD.

IN TWO VOLUMES.

VOL. I.

LONDON:

EDWARD MOXON, DOVER STREET.

MDCCCXLVI.

LONDON:
BRADBURY AND EVANS, PRINTERS, WHITEFRIARS.

PREFACE.

—•—

THIS collection of Mr. Hood's serious Poems is made in fulfilment of his own desire. It was among his last instructions to those who were dearest to him.

If its reception should justify the earnest hope which the writer had allowed himself to entertain, it will be followed by a volume composed of the more thoughtful pieces in his Poems of wit and humour.

It is believed that the most sacred duty which his friends owed to his memory will thus have been discharged ; and that in any future recital of the names of writers who have contributed to the stock of genuine English Poetry, Thomas Hood will find honourable mention.

Some minor pieces printed for the first time are placed at the commencement of the Second Volume.

December, 1845.

CONTENTS

OF

VOLUME THE FIRST.

— ◆ —

POEMS.

✦

THE DREAM OF EUGENE ARAM.

'Twas in the prime of summer time,
    An evening calm and cool,
And four-and-twenty happy boys
    Came bounding out of school :
There were some that ran and some that leapt,
    Like troutlets in a pool.

Away they sped with gamesome minds,
    And souls untouched by sin ;
To a level mead they came, and there
    They drave the wickets in :
Pleasantly shone the setting sun
    Over the town of Lynn.

Like sportive deer they cours'd about,
    And shouted as they ran,—
Turning to mirth all things of earth,
    As only boyhood can ;
But the Usher sat remote from all,
    A melancholy man !

His hat was off, his vest apart,
    To catch heaven's blessed breeze ;
For a burning thought was in his brow,
    And his bosom ill at ease :
So he lean'd his head on his hands, and read
    The book between his knees !

Leaf after leaf he turn'd it o'er,
    Nor ever glanc'd aside,
For the peace of his soul he read that book
    In the golden eventide :
Much study had made him very lean,
    And pale, and leaden-ey'd.

At last he shut the ponderous tome,
  With a fast and fervent grasp
He strain'd the dusky covers close,
  And fix'd the brazen hasp :
" Oh, God ! could I so close my mind,
  And clasp it with a clasp ! "

Then leaping on his feet upright,
  Some moody turns he took,—
Now up the mead, then down the mead,
  And past a shady nook,—
And, lo ! he saw a little boy
  That pored upon a book !

" My gentle lad, what is 't you read—
  Romance or fairy fable ? ·
Or is it some historic page,
  Of kings and crowns unstable ? "
The young boy gave an upward glance,—
  " It is ' The Death of Abel.' "

The Usher took six hasty strides,
　　As smit with sudden pain,—
Six hasty strides beyond the place,
　　Then slowly back again ;
And down he sat beside the lad,
　　And talk'd with him of Cain ;

And, long since then, of bloody men,
　　Whose deeds tradition saves ;
Of lonely folk cut off unseen,
　　And hid in sudden graves ;
Of horrid stabs, in groves forlorn,
　　And murders done in caves ;

And how the sprites of injur'd men
　　Shriek upward from the sod,—
Aye, how the ghostly hand will point
　　To shew the burial clod ;
And unknown facts of guilty acts
　　Are seen in dreams from God !

He told how murderers walk the earth
    Beneath the curse of Cain,—
With crimson clouds before their eyes,
    And flames about their brain :
For blood has left upon their souls
    Its everlasting stain !

" And well," quoth he, " I know, for truth,
    Their pangs must be extreme,—
Woe, woe, unutterable woe,—
    Who spill life's sacred stream !
For why ? Methought, last night, I wrought
    A murder, in a dream !

" One that had never done me wrong—
    A feeble man, and old :
I led him to a lonely field,—
    The moon shone clear and cold :
Now here, said I, this man shall die,
    And I will have his gold !

" Two sudden blows with a ragged stick,
    And one with a heavy stone,
One hurried gash with a hasty knife,—
    And then the deed was done :
There was nothing lying at my foot
    But lifeless flesh and bone !

" Nothing but lifeless flesh and bone,
    That could not do me ill ;
And yet I fear'd him all the more,
    For lying there so still :
There was a manhood in his look,
    That murder could not kill !

" And, lo ! the universal air
    Seem'd lit with ghastly flame ;—
Ten thousand thousand dreadful eyes
    Were looking down in blame :
I took the dead man by his hand,
    And call'd upon his name !

" Oh, God ! it made me quake to see
  Such sense within the slain !
But when I touch'd the lifeless clay,
  The blood gushed out amain !
For every clot, a burning spot
  Was scorching in my brain !

" My head was like an ardent coal,
  My heart as solid ice ;
My wretched, wretched soul, I knew,
  Was at the Devil's price :
A dozen times I groan'd ; the dead
  Had never groan'd but twice !

" And now, from forth the frowning sky,
  From the Heaven's topmost height,
I heard a voice—the awful voice
  Of the blood-avenging sprite :—
' Thou guilty man ! take up thy dead
  And hide it from my sight ! '

" I took the dreary body up,
　　And cast it in a stream,—
A sluggish water, black as ink,
　　The depth was so extreme :—
My gentle Boy, remember this
　　Is nothing but a dream !

" Down went the corse with a hollow plunge,
　　And vanish'd in the pool ;
Anon I cleans'd my bloody hands,
　　And wash'd my forehead cool.
And sat among the urchins young,
　　That evening in the school.

" Oh, Heaven ! to think of their white souls,
　　And mine so black and grim !
I could not share in childish prayer,
　　Nor join in Evening Hymn :
Like a Devil of the Pit I seem'd,
　　'Mid holy Cherubim !

" And peace went with them, one and all,
　　And each calm pillow spread;
But Guilt was my grim Chamberlain
　　That lighted me to bed;
And drew my midnight curtains round,
　　With fingers bloody red!

" All night I lay in agony,
　　In anguish dark and deep;
My fever'd eyes I dared not close,
　　But stared aghast at Sleep:
For Sin had render'd unto her
　　The keys of Hell to keep!

" All night I lay in agony,
　　From weary chime to chime,
With one besetting horrid hint,
　　That rack'd me all the time;
A mighty yearning, like the first
　　Fierce impulse unto crime!

" One stern tyrannic thought, that made
    All other thoughts its slave;
Stronger and stronger every pulse
    Did that temptation crave,—
Still urging me to go and see
    The Dead Man in his grave!

" Heavily I rose up, as soon
    As light was in the sky,
And sought the black accursed pool
    With a wild misgiving eye;
And I saw the Dead in the river bed,
    For the faithless stream was dry!

" Merrily rose the lark, and shook
    The dew-drop from its wing;
But I never mark'd its morning flight,
    I never heard it sing:
For I was stooping once again
    Under the horrid thing.

" With breathless speed, like a soul in chase,
　　I took him up and ran ;—
There was no time to dig a grave
　　Before the day began :
In a lonesome wood, with heaps of leaves,
　　I hid the murder'd man !

" And all that day I read in school,
　　But my thought was other where ;
As soon as the mid-day task was done,
　　In secret I was there :
And a mighty wind had swept the leaves,
　　And still the corse was bare !

" Then down I cast me on my face,
　　And first began to weep,
For I knew my secret then was one
　　That earth refused to keep :
Or land or sea, though he should be
　　Ten thousand fathoms deep.

" So wills the fierce avenging Sprite,
    Till blood for blood atones !
Ay, though he 's buried in a cave,
    And trodden down with stones,
And years have rotted off his flesh,—
    The world shall see his bones !

" Oh, God ! that horrid, horrid dream
    Besets me now awake !
Again—again, with dizzy brain,
    The human life I take ;
And my red right hand grows raging hot,
    Like Cranmer's at the stake.

" And still no peace for the restless clay,
    Will wave or mould allow ;
The horrid thing pursues my soul,—
    It stands before me now !"
The fearful Boy look'd up, and saw
    Huge drops upon his brow.

That very night, while gentle sleep
  The urchin eyelids kiss'd,
Two stern-faced men set out from Lynn,
  Through the cold and heavy mist;
And Eugene Aram walked between,
  With gyves upon his wrist.

THE ELM TREE:

A DREAM IN THE WOODS.

And this our life, exempt from public haunt,
Finds tongues in trees.

As You Like It.

'Twas in a shady Avenue,

Where lofty Elms abound—

And from a Tree

There came to me

A sad and solemn sound,

That sometimes murmur'd overhead,

And sometimes underground.

Amongst the leaves it seem'd to sigh.

Amid the boughs to moan;

It mutter'd in the stem, and then

The roots took up the tone;

As if beneath the dewy grass

The dead began to groan.

No breeze there was to stir the leaves;
  No bolts that tempests launch,
To rend the trunk or rugged bark;
  No gale to bend the branch:
No quake of earth to heave the roots,
  That stood so stiff and staunch.

No bird was preening up aloft,
  To rustle with its wing;
No squirrel, in its sport or fear,
  From bough to bough to spring;
    The solid bole
    Had ne'er a hole
To hide a living thing!

No scooping hollow cell to lodge
  A furtive beast or fowl,
    The martin, bat,
    Or forest cat
That nightly loves to prowl,
Nor ivy nook so apt to shroud
  The moping, snoring owl.

But still the sound was in my ear,
   A sad and solemn sound,
That sometimes murmur'd overhead,
   And sometimes underground—
'Twas in a shady Avenue
   Where lofty Elms abound.

O hath the Dryad still a tongue
   In this ungenial clime ?
Have Sylvan Spirits still a voice
   As in the classic prime—
To make the forest voluble,
   As in the olden time ?

The olden time is dead and gone ;
   Its years have fill'd their sum—
And e'en in Greece—her native Greece—
   The Sylvan Nymph is dumb—
From ash, and beech, and aged oak,
   No classic whispers come.

From Poplar, Pine, and drooping Birch,
   And fragrant Linden Trees ;
      No living sound
      E'er hovers round,
   Unless the vagrant breeze,
The music of the merry bird,
   Or hum of busy bees.

But busy bees forsake the Elm
   That bears no bloom aloft—
The Finch was in the hawthorn-bush,
   The Blackbird in the croft ;
And among the firs the brooding Dove,
   That else might murmur soft.

Yet still I heard that solemn sound,
   And sad it was to boot,
From ev'ry overhanging bough,
   And each minuter shoot ;
From the rugged trunk and mossy rind
   And from the twisted root.

From these,—a melancholy moan :
    From those,—a dreary sigh ;
As if the boughs were wintry bare,
    And wild winds sweeping by—
Whereas the smallest fleecy cloud
    Was steadfast in the sky.

No sign or touch of stirring air
    Could either sense observe—
The zephyr had not breath enough
    The thistle-down to swerve,
Or force the filmy gossamers
    To take another curve.

In still and silent slumber hush'd
    All Nature seem'd to be :
From heaven above, or earth beneath,
    No whisper came to me—
Except the solemn sound and sad
    From that MYSTERIOUS TREE !

A hollow, hollow, hollow sound,
 As is that dreamy roar
When distant billows boil and bound
 Along a shingly shore—
But the ocean brim was far aloof,
 A hundred miles or more.

No murmur of the gusty sea,
 No tumult of the beach,
However they might foam and fret,
 The bounded sense could reach—
Methought the trees in mystic tongue
 Were talking each to each !—

Mayhap, rehearsing ancient tales
 Of greenwood love or guilt,
 Of whisper'd vows
 Beneath their boughs :
 Or blood obscurely spilt ;
Or of that near-hand Mansion House
 A Royal Tudor built.

Perchance, of booty won or shared
 Beneath the starry cope—
Or where the suicidal wretch
 Hung up the fatal rope ;
Or Beauty kept an evil tryste,
 Insnared by Love and Hope.

Of graves, perchance, untimely scoop'd
 At midnight dark and dank—
And what is underneath the sod
 Whereon the grass is rank—
  Of old intrigues,
   And privy leagues,
 Tradition leaves in blank.

Of traitor lips that mutter'd plots—
 Of Kin who fought and fell—
God knows the undiscover'd schemes.
 The arts and acts of Hell,
Perform'd long generations since,
 If trees had tongues to tell !

With wary eyes, and ears alert,
　　As one who walks afraid,
I wander'd down the dappled path
　　Of mingled light and shade—
How sweetly gleam'd that arch of blue
　　Beyond the green arcade !

How cheerly shone the glimpse of Heav'n
　　Beyond that verdant aisle !
All overarch'd with lofty elms,
　　That quench'd the light, the while,
　　　　As dim and chill
　　　　As serves to fill
　　Some old Cathedral pile !

And many a gnarlèd trunk was there,
　　That ages long had stood,
Till Time had wrought them into shapes
　　Like Pan's fantastic brood ;
Or still more foul and hideous forms
　　That Pagans carve in wood !

A crouching Satyr lurking here—
  And there a Goblin grim—
As staring full of demon life
  As Gothic sculptor's whim—
A marvel it had scarcely been
  To hear a voice from him !

Some whisper from that horrid mouth
  Of strange, unearthly tone ;
Or wild infernal laugh, to chill
  One's marrow in the bone.
But no——it grins like rigid Death,
  And silent as a stone !

As silent as its fellows be,
  For all is mute with them—
The branch that climbs the leafy roof—
  The rough and mossy stem—
      The crooked root,
      And tender shoot,
Where hangs the dewy gem.

One mystic Tree alone there is,
  Of sad and solemn sound—
That sometimes murmurs overhead,
  And sometimes underground—
In all that shady Avenue,
  Where lofty Elms abound.

PART II.

THE Scene is changed ! No green Arcade—
  No Trees all ranged a-row—
But scatter'd like a beaten host,
  Dispersing to and fro ;
With here and there a sylvan corse,
  That fell before the foe.

The Foe that down in yonder dell
  Pursues his daily toil :
As witness many a prostrate trunk,
  Bereft of leafy spoil,
Hard by its wooden stump, whereon
  The adder loves to coil.

Alone he works—his ringing blows
    Have banish'd bird and beast ;
The Hind and Fawn have canter'd off
    A hundred yards at least ;
And on the maple's lofty top,
    The linnet's song has ceased.

No eye his labour overlooks,
    Or when he takes his rest ;
Except the timid thrush that peeps
    Above her secret nest,
Forbid by love to leave the young
    Beneath her speckled breast.

The Woodman's heart is in his work,
    His axe is sharp and good :
With sturdy arm and steady aim
    He smites the gaping wood ;
      From distant rocks
      His lusty knocks
Re-echo many a rood.

His axe is keen, his arm is strong :
    The muscles serve him well ;
His years have reach'd an extra span,
    The number none can tell ;
But still his lifelong task has been
    The Timber Tree to fell.

Through Summer's parching sultriness.
    And Winter's freezing cold,
        From sapling youth
        To virile growth,
    And Age's rigid mould,
His energetic axe hath rung
    Within that Forest old.

Aloft, upon his poising steel
    The vivid sunbeams glance—
About his head and round his feet
    The forest shadows dance ;
And bounding from his russet coat
    The acorn drops askance.

His face is like a Druid's face,
  With wrinkles furrow'd deep,
And tann'd by scorching suns as brown
  As corn that's ripe to reap ;
But the hair on brow, and cheek, and chin,
  Is white as wool of sheep.

His frame is like a giant's frame ;
  His legs are long and stark ;
His arms like limbs of knotted yew ;
  His hands like rugged bark ;
        So he felleth still
        With right good will,
  As if to build an Ark !

Oh ! well within *His* fatal path
  The fearful Tree might quake
Through every fibre, twig, and leaf,
  With aspen tremour shake ;
        Through trunk and root,
        And branch and shoot,
  A low complaining make !

Oh ! well to *Him* the Tree might breathe
    A sad and solemn sound,
A sigh that murmur'd overhead,
    And groans from underground ;
As in that shady Avenue
    Where lofty Elms abound !

But calm and mute the Maple stands,
    The Plane, the Ash, the Fir,
The Elm, the Beech, the drooping Birch,
    Without the least demur ;
And e'en the Aspen's hoary leaf
    Makes no unusual stir.

The Pines—those old gigantic Pines,
    That writhe—recalling soon
The famous Human Group that writhes
    With Snakes in wild festoon—
In ramous wrestlings interlaced
    A Forest Läocoon—

Like Titans of primeval girth
　　By tortures overcome,
Their brown enormous limbs they twine
　　Bedew'd with tears of gum—
Fierce agonies that ought to yell,
　　But, like the marble, dumb.

Nay, yonder blasted Elm that stands
　　So like a man of sin,
Who, frantic, flings his arms abroad
　　To feel the Worm within—
For all that gesture, so intense,
　　It makes no sort of din !

An universal silence reigns
　　In rugged bark or peel,
Except that very trunk which rings
　　Beneath the biting steel—
Meanwhile the Woodman plies his axe
　　With unrelenting zeal !

No rustic song is on his tongue,
    No whistle on his lips ;
But with a quiet thoughtfulness
    His trusty tool he grips,
And, stroke on stroke, keeps hacking out
    The bright and flying chips.

Stroke after stroke, with frequent dint
    He spreads the fatal gash ;
Till lo ! the remnant fibres rend,
    With harsh and sudden crash,
And on the dull resounding turf
    The jarring branches lash !

Oh ! now the Forest Trees may sigh.
    The Ash, the Poplar tall,
The Elm, the Birch, the drooping Beech.
    The Aspens—one and all,
        With solemn groan
        And hollow moan
    Lament a comrade's fall !

A goodly Elm, of noble girth,
    That, thrice the human span—
While on their variegated course
    The constant Seasons ran—
Through gale, and hail, and fiery bolt,
    Had stood erect as Man.

But now, like mortal Man himself,
    Struck down by hand of God,
Or heathen Idol tumbled prone
    Beneath th' Eternal's nod,
In all its giant bulk and length
    It lies along the sod !—

Ay, now the Forest Trees may grieve
    And make a common moan
Around that patriarchal trunk
    So newly overthrown :
And with a murmur recognise
    A doom to be their own !

The Echo sleeps : the idle axe.
    A disregarded tool,
Lies crushing with its passive weight
    The toad's reputed stool—
The Woodman wipes his dewy brow
    Within the shadows cool.

No Zephyr stirs : the ear may catch
    The smallest insect-hum ;
But on the disappointed sense
    No mystic whispers come ;
No tone of sylvan sympathy,
    The Forest Trees are dumb.

No leafy noise, nor inward voice,
    No sad and solemn sound,
That sometimes murmurs overhead,
    And sometimes underground :
As in that shady Avenue,
    Where lofty Elms abound !

PART III.

THE deed is done : the Tree is low
    That stood so long and firm ;
The Woodman and his axe are gone,
    His toil has found its term ;
And where he wrought the speckled Thrush
    Securely hunts the worm.

The Cony from the sandy bank
    Has run a rapid race,
Through thistle, bent, and tangled fern,
    To seek the open space ;
And on its haunches sits erect
    To clean its furry face.

The dappled Fawn is close at hand,
    The Hind is browsing near,—
And on the Larch's lowest bough
    The Ousel whistles clear ;
      But checks the note
      Within his throat,
As choked with sudden fear !

With sudden fear her wormy quest
    The Thrush abruptly quits—
Through thistle, bent, and tangled fern
    The startled Cony flits;
And on the Larch's lowest bough
    No more the Ousel sits.

        With sudden fear
        The dappled Deer
    Effect a swift escape:
But well might bolder creatures start,
    And fly, or stand agape,
With rising hair, and curdled blood,
    To see so grim a Shape!

    The very sky turns pale above:
        The earth grows dark beneath;
    The human Terror thrills with cold,
        And draws a shorter breath—
    An universal panic owns
        The dread approach of DEATH!

With silent pace, as shadows come,
    And dark as shadows be,
The grisly Phantom takes his stand
    Beside the fallen Tree,
And scans it with his gloomy eyes,
    And laughs with horrid glee—

A dreary laugh and desolate,
    Where mirth is void and null,
As hollow as its echo sounds
    Within the hollow skull—
" Whoever laid this tree along
    His hatchet was not dull !

" The human arm and human tool
    Have done their duty well !
But after sound of ringing axe
    Must sound the ringing knell :
        When Elm or Oak
        Have felt the stroke
    My turn it is to fell !

" No passive unregarded tree,
    A senseless thing of wood,
Wherein the sluggish sap ascends
    To swell the vernal bud—
But conscious, moving, breathing trunks
    That throb with living blood !

" No forest Monarch yearly clad
    In mantle green or brown ;
That unrecorded lives, and falls
    By hand of rustic clown—
But Kings who don the purple robe,
    And wear the jewell'd crown.

" Ah ! little recks the Royal mind,
    Within his Banquet Hall,
While tapers shine and Music breathes
    And Beauty leads the Ball,—
He little recks the oaken plank
    Shall be his palace wall !

" Ah, little dreams the haughty Peer,
    The while his Falcon flies—
Or on the blood-bedabbled turf
    The antler'd quarry dies—
That in his own ancestral Park
    The narrow dwelling lies !

" But haughty Peer and mighty King
    One doom shall overwhelm !
            The oaken cell
            Shall lodge him well
    Whose sceptre ruled a realm—
While he who never knew a home,
    Shall find it in the Elm !

" The tatter'd, lean, dejected wretch,
    Who begs from door to door,
And dies within the cressy ditch,
    Or on the barren moor,
The friendly Elm shall lodge and clothe
    That houseless man, and poor !

" Yea, this recumbent rugged trunk,
　　That lies so long and prone,
With many a fallen acorn-cup,
　　And mast, and firry cone—
This rugged trunk shall hold its share
　　Of mortal flesh and bone !

" A Miser hoarding heaps of gold,
　　But pale with ague-fears—
A Wife lamenting love's decay,
　　With secret cruel tears,
Distilling bitter, bitter drops
　　From sweets of former years—

" A Man within whose gloomy mind,
　　Offence had darkly sunk,
Who out of fierce Revenge's cup
　　Hath madly, darkly drunk—
Grief, Avarice, and Hate shall sleep
　　Within this very trunk !

" This massy trunk that lies along,
        And many more must fall—
            For the very knave
            Who digs the grave,
        The man who spreads the pall,
    And he who tolls the funeral bell,
        The Elm shall have them all !

" The tall abounding Elm that grows
        In hedgerows up and down ;
    In field and forest, copse and park,
        And in the peopled town,
    With colonies of noisy rooks
        That nestle on its crown.

" And well th' abounding Elm may grow
        In field and hedge so rife,
    In forest, copse, and wooded park,
        And mid the city's strife,
    For, every hour that passes by,
        Shall end a human life !"

The Phantom ends : the shade is gone ;
   The sky is clear and bright ;
On turf, and moss, and fallen Tree,
   There glows a ruddy light :
And bounding through the golden fern
   The Rabbit comes to bite.

The Thrush's mate beside her sits
   And pipes a merry lay ;
The Dove is in the evergreens ;
   And on the Larch's spray
The Fly-bird flutters up and down,
   To catch its tiny prey.

The gentle Hind and dappled Fawn
   Are coming up the glade :
Each harmless furr'd and feather'd thing
   Is glad, and not afraid—
But on my sadden'd spirit still
   The Shadow leaves a shade.

A secret, vague, prophetic gloom,
　　As though by certain mark
I knew the fore-appointed Tree,
　　Within whose rugged bark
This warm and living frame shall find
　　Its narrow house and dark.

That mystic Tree which breathed to me
　　A sad and solemn sound,
That sometimes murmur'd overhead
　　And sometimes underground;
Within that shady Avenue
　　Where lofty Elms abound.

THE HAUNTED HOUSE.

A ROMANCE.

.

" A jolly place," said he, " in times of old !
But something ails it now : the place is curst."
HART-LEAP WELL, BY WORDSWORTH.

PART I.

SOME dreams we have are nothing else but dreams,

Unnatural, and full of contradictions ;

Yet others of our most romantic schemes

Are something more than fictions.

It might be only on enchanted ground :

It might be merely by a thought's expansion ;

But in the spirit, or the flesh, I found

An old deserted Mansion.

A residence for woman, child, and man,
A dwelling place,—and yet no habitation ;
A House,—but under some prodigious ban
Of excommunication.

Unhinged the iron gates half open hung,
Jarr'd by the gusty gales of many winters,
That from its crumbled pedestal had flung
One marble globe in splinters.

No dog was at the threshold, great or small ;
No pigeon on the roof—no household creature—
No cat demurely dozing on the wall—
Not one domestic feature.

No human figure stirr'd, to go or come,
No face look'd forth from shut or open casement ;
No chimney smoked—there was no sign of Home
From parapet to basement.

With shatter'd panes the grassy court was starr'd;
The time-worn coping-stone had tumbled after;
And through the ragged roof the sky shone, barr'd
With naked beam and rafter.

O'er all there hung a shadow and a fear;
A sense of mystery the spirit daunted,
And said, as plain as whisper in the ear,
The place is Haunted!

The flow'r grew wild and rankly as the weed,
Roses with thistles struggled for espial,
And vagrant plants of parasitic breed
Had overgrown the Dial

But gay or gloomy, steadfast or infirm,
No heart was there to heed the hour's duration;
All times and tides were lost in one long term
Of stagnant desolation.

The wren had built within the Porch, she found
Its quiet loneliness so sure and thorough;
And on the lawn,—within its turfy mound,—
The rabbit made his burrow.

The rabbit wild and gray, that flitted through
The shrubby clumps, and frisk'd, and sat, and vanish'd,
But leisurely and bold, as if he knew
His enemy was banish'd.

The wary crow,—the pheasant from the woods—
Lull'd by the still and everlasting sameness,
Close to the Mansion, like domestic broods,
Fed with a " shocking tameness."

The coot was swimming in the reedy pond,
Beside the water-hen, so soon affrighted;
And in the weedy moat the heron, fond
Of solitude, alighted.

The moping heron, motionless and stiff,
That on a stone, as silently and stilly,
Stood, an apparent sentinel, as if
To guard the water-lily.

No sound was heard except, from far away,
The ringing of the Whitwall's shrilly laughter,
Or, now and then, the chatter of the jay,
That Echo murmur'd after.

But Echo never mock'd the human tongue;
Some weighty crime, that Heaven could not pardon,
A secret curse on that old Building hung,
And its deserted Garden.

The beds were all untouch'd by hand or tool;
No footstep marked the damp and mossy gravel,
Each walk as green as is the mantled pool,
For want of human travel.

The vine unprun'd, and the neglected peach,
Droop'd from the wall with which they used to grapple :
And on the canker'd tree, in easy reach.
Rotted the golden apple.

But awfully the truant shunn'd the ground,
The vagrant kept aloof, and daring Poacher ;
In spite of gaps that through the fences round
Invited the encroacher.

For over all there hung a cloud of fear.
A sense of mystery the spirit daunted.
And said, as plain as whisper in the ear,
The place is Haunted !

The pear and quince lay squander'd on the grass :
The mould was purple with unheeded showers
Of bloomy plums—a Wilderness it was
Of fruits, and weeds. and flowers !

The marigold amidst the nettles blew,
The gourd embraced the rose bush in its ramble,
The thistle and the stock together grew,
The holly-hock and bramble.

The bear-bine with the lilac interlac'd,
The sturdy bur-dock choked its slender neighbour,
The spicy pink.   All tokens were effac'd
Of human care and labour.

The very yew Formality had train'd
To such a rigid pyramidal stature,
For want of trimming had almost regain'd
The raggedness of nature.

The Fountain was a-dry—neglect and time
Had marr'd the work of artisan and mason,
And efts and croaking frogs, begot of slime,
Sprawl'd in the ruin'd bason.

The Statue, fallen from its marble base,
Amidst the refuse leaves, and herbage rotten,
Lay like the Idol of some by-gone race,
Its name and rites forgotten.

On ev'ry side the aspect was the same,
All ruin'd, desolate, forlorn, and savage:
No hand or foot within the precinct came
To rectify or ravage.

For over all there hung a cloud of fear,
A sense of mystery the spirit daunted,
And said as plain as whisper in the ear,
The place is Haunted !

PART II

O, VERY gloomy is the House of Woe,
Where tears are falling while the bell is knelling,
With all the dark solemnities which show
That Death is in the dwelling !

O very, very dreary is the room
Where Love, domestic Love, no longer nestles,
But smitten by the common stroke of doom,
The Corpse lies on the trestles !

But House of Woe, and hearse, and sable pall,
The narrow home of the departed mortal,
Ne'er look'd so gloomy as that Ghostly Hall,
With its deserted portal !

The centipede along the threshold crept,
The cobweb hung across in mazy tangle,
And in its winding-sheet the maggot slept,
At every nook and angle.

The keyhole lodged the earwig and her brood.
The emmets of the steps had old possession,
And march'd in search of their diurnal food
In undisturb'd procession.

As undisturb'd as the prehensile cell
Of moth or maggot, or the spider's tissue,
For never foot upon that threshold fell,
To enter or to issue.

O'er all there hung the shadow of a fear,
A sense of mystery the spirit daunted,
And said, as plain as whisper in the ear,
The place is Haunted.

Howbeit, the door I push'd—or so I dream'd—
Which slowly, slowly gaped,—the hinges creaking
With such a rusty eloquence, it seem'd
That Time himself was speaking.

But Time was dumb within that Mansion old,
Or left his tale to the heraldic banners
That hung from the corroded walls, and told
Of former men and manners.

Those tatter'd flags, that with the open'd door,
Seem'd the old wave of battle to remember,
While fallen fragments danced upon the floor
Like dead leaves in December.

The startled bats flew out—bird after bird—
The screech-owl overhead began to flutter,
And seem'd to mock the cry that she had heard
Some dying victim utter!

A shriek that echoed from the joisted roof,
And up the stair, and further still and further,
Till in some ringing chamber far aloof
It ceased its tale of murther!

Meanwhile the rusty armour rattled round,
The banner shudder'd, and the ragged streamer;
All things the horrid tenor of the sound
Acknowledged with a tremor.

The antlers, where the helmet hung and belt,
Stirr'd as the tempest stirs the forest branches,
Or as the stag had trembled when he felt
The blood-hound at his haunches.

The window jingled in its crumbled frame,
And thro' its many gaps of destitution
Dolorous moans and hollow sighings came,
Like those of dissolution.

The wood-louse dropp'd, and rolled into a ball,
Touch'd by some impulse occult or mechanic;
And nameless beetles ran along the wall
In universal panic.

The subtle spider, that from overhead
Hung like a spy on human guilt and error,
Suddenly turn'd, and up its slender thread
Ran with a nimble terror.

The very stains and fractures on the wall
Assuming features solemn and terrific,
Hinted some Tragedy of that old Hall,
Lock'd up in hieroglyphic.

Some tale that might, perchance, have solved the doubt,
Wherefore amongst those flags so dull and livid,
The banner of the BLOODY HAND shone out
So ominously vivid.

Some key to that inscrutable appeal,
Which made the very frame of Nature quiver ;
And ev'ry thrilling nerve and fibre feel
So ague-like a shiver.

For over all there hung a cloud of fear,
A sense of mystery the spirit daunted;
And said, as plain as whisper in the ear,
The place is Haunted!

If but a rat had linger'd in the house,
To lure the thought into a social channel!
But not a rat remain'd, or tiny mouse,
To squeak behind the pannel.

Huge drops roll'd down the walls, as if they wept;
And where the cricket used to chirp so shrilly,
The toad was squatting, and the lizard crept
On that damp hearth and chilly.

For years no cheerful blaze had sparkled there,
Or glanced on coat of buff or knightly metal;
The slug was crawling on the vacant chair,—
The snail upon the settle.

The floor was redolent of mould and must,
The fungus in the rotten seams had quicken'd;
While on the oaken table coats of dust
Perennially had thicken'd.

No mark of leathern jack or metal cann,
No cup—no horn—no hospitable token,—
All social ties between that board and Man
Had long ago been broken.

There was so foul a rumour in the air,
The shadow of a Presence so atrocious ;
No human creature could have feasted there,
Even the most ferocious.

For over all there hung a cloud of fear,
A sense of mystery the spirit daunted,
And said, as plain as whisper in the ear,
The place is Haunted !

PART III

'Tis hard for human actions to account,
Whether from reason or from impulse only—
But some internal prompting bade me mount
The gloomy stairs and lonely.

Those gloomy stairs, so dark, and damp, and cold,
With odours as from bones and relics carnal,
Deprived of rite, and consecrated mould,
The chapel vault, or charnel.

Those dreary stairs, where with the sounding stress
Of ev'ry step so many echoes blended,
The mind, with dark misgivings, fear'd to guess
How many feet ascended.

The tempest with its spoils had drifted in,
Till each unwholesome stone was darkly spotted,
As thickly as the leopard's dappled skin,
With leaves that rankly rotted.

The air was thick—and in the upper gloom
The bat—or something in its shape—was winging :
And on the wall, as chilly as a tomb,
The Death's-Head moth was clinging.

That mystic moth, which, with a sense profound
Of all unholy presence, augurs truly ;
And with a grim significance flits round
The taper burning bluely.

Such omens in the place there seem'd to be,
At ev'ry crooked turn, or on the landing,
The straining eyeball was prepared to see
Some Apparition standing.

For over all there hung a cloud of fear,
A sense of mystery the spirit daunted,
And said, as plain as whisper in the ear,
The place is Haunted !

Yet no portentous Shape the sight amazed ;
Each object plain, and tangible, and valid ;
But from their tarnish'd frames dark Figures gazed,
And Faces spectre-pallid.

Not merely with the mimic life that lies
Within the compass of Art's simulation :
Their souls were looking thro' their painted eyes
With awful speculation.

On ev'ry lip a speechless horror dwelt ;
On ev'ry brow the burthen of affliction ;
The old Ancestral Spirits knew and felt
The House's malediction.

Such earnest woe their features overcast,
They might have stirr'd, or sigh'd, or wept, or spoken :
But, save the hollow moaning of the blast,
The stillness was unbroken.

No other sound or stir of life was there,
Except my steps in solitary clamber,
From flight to flight, from humid stair to stair,
From chamber into chamber.

Deserted rooms of luxury and state,
That old magnificence had richly furnish'd
With pictures, cabinets of ancient date,
And carvings gilt and burnish'd.

Rich hangings, storied by the needle's art,
With scripture history, or classic fable ;
But all had faded, save one ragged part,
Where Cain was slaying Abel.

The silent waste of mildew and the moth
Had marr'd the tissue with a partial ravage ;
But undecaying frown'd upon the cloth
Each feature stern and savage.

The sky was pale ; the cloud a thing of doubt :
Some hues were fresh, and some decay'd and duller ;
But still the BLOODY HAND shone strangely out
With vehemence of colour !

The BLOODY HAND that with a lurid stain
Shone on the dusty floor, a dismal token,
Projected from the casement's painted pane,
Where all beside was broken.

The BLOODY HAND significant of crime,
That glaring on the old heraldic banner,
Had kept its crimson unimpair'd by time,
In such a wondrous manner !

O'er all there hung the shadow of a fear,
A sense of mystery the spirit daunted,
And said, as plain as whisper in the ear,
The place is Haunted !

The Death Watch tick'd behind the pannel'd oak,
Inexplicable tremors shook the arras,
And echoes strange and mystical awoke,
The fancy to embarrass,

Prophetic hints that fill'd the soul with dread,
But thro' one gloomy entrance pointing mostly,
The while some secret inspiration said,
That Chamber is the Ghostly !

Across the door no gossamer festoon
Swung pendulous—no web—no dusty fringes,
No silky chrysalis or white cocoon
About its nooks and hinges.

The spider shunn'd the interdicted room,
The moth, the beetle, and the fly were banish'd,
And where the sunbeam fell athwart the gloom
The very midge had vanish'd.

One lonely ray that glanced upon a Bed,
As if with awful aim direct and certain,
To show the BLOODY HAND in burning red
Embroider'd on the curtain.

And yet no gory stain was on the quilt—
The pillow in its place had slowly rotted ;
The floor alone retain'd the trace of guilt,
Those boards obscurely spotted.

Obscurely spotted to the door, and thence
With mazy doubles to the grated casement—
Oh what a tale they told of fear intense,
Of horror and amazement !

What human creature in the dead of night
Had coursed like hunted hare that cruel distance ?
Had sought the door, the window in his flight,
Striving for dear existence ?

What shrieking Spirit in that bloody room
Its mortal frame had violently quitted?—
Across the sunbeam, with a sudden gloom,
A ghostly Shadow flitted.

Across the sunbeam, and along the wall,
But painted on the air so very dimly,
It hardly veil'd the tapestry at all,
Or portrait frowning grimly.

O'er all there hung the shadow of a fear,
A sense of mystery the spirit daunted,
And said, as plain as whisper in the ear,
The place is Haunted!

THE BRIDGE OF SIGHS.

" Drown'd ! drown'd ! "—HAMLET.

ONE more Unfortunate,
Weary of breath,
Rashly importunate,
Gone to her death !

Take her up tenderly,
Lift her with care ;
Fashion'd so slenderly,
Young, and so fair !

Look at her garments
Clinging like cerements :
Whilst the wave constantly
Drips from her clothing ;
Take her up instantly,
Loving, not loathing.—

Touch her not scornfully ;
Think of her mournfully,
Gently and humanly ;
Not of the stains of her,
All that remains of her
Now is pure womanly.

Make no deep scrutiny
Into her mutiny
Rash and undutiful :
Past all dishonour,
Death has left on her
Only the beautiful.

Still, for all slips of hers,
One of Eve's family—
Wipe those poor lips of hers
Oozing so clammily.

Loop up her tresses
Escaped from the comb,
Her fair auburn tresses ;

Whilst wonderment guesses
Where was her home ?

Who was her father ?
Who was her mother ?
Had she a sister ?
Had she a brother ?
Or was there a dearer one
Still, and a nearer one
Yet, than all other ?

Alas ! for the rarity
Of Christian charity
Under the sun !
Oh ! it was pitiful !
Near a whole city full,
Home she had none.

Sisterly, brotherly,
Fatherly, motherly
Feelings had changed :
Love, by harsh evidence,

Thrown from its eminence ;
Even God's providence
Seeming estranged.

Where the lamps quiver
So far in the river,
With many a light
From window and casement.
From garret to basement,
She stood, with amazement.
Houseless by night.

The bleak wind of March
Made her tremble and shiver :
But not the dark arch,
Or the black flowing river :
Mad from life's history,
Glad to death's mystery,
Swift to be hurl'd—
Any where, any where
Out of the world !

In she plunged boldly,
No matter how coldly
The rough river ran,—
Over the brink of it,
Picture it—think of it.
Dissolute Man !
Lave in it, drink of it.
Then, if you can !

Take her up tenderly.
Lift her with care :
Fashion'd so slenderly,
Young, and so fair !

Ere her limbs frigidly
Stiffen too rigidly,
Decently,—kindly,—
Smoothe, and compose them :
And her eyes, close them.
Staring so blindly !

Dreadfully staring
Thro' muddy impurity,

As when with the daring
Last look of despairing
Fix'd on futurity.

Perishing gloomily,
Spurr'd by contumely,
Cold inhumanity,
Burning insanity,
Into her rest.—
Cross her hands humbly,
As if praying dumbly,
Over her breast !

Owning her weakness,
Her evil behaviour,
And leaving, with meekness,
Her sins to her Saviour !

THE SONG OF THE SHIRT.

WITH fingers weary and worn,
　With eyelids heavy and red,
A woman sat, in unwomanly rags,
　Plying her needle and thread—
　　Stitch ! stitch ! stitch !
In poverty, hunger, and dirt,
　And still with a voice of dolorous pitch
She sang the " Song of the Shirt ! "

　" Work ! work ! work !
While the cock is crowing aloof !
　And work—work—work,
Till the stars shine through the roof !
It 's O ! to be a slave
　Along with the barbarous Turk,
Where woman has never a soul to save.
　If this is Christian work !

" Work—work—work
Till the brain begins to swim ;
Work—work—work
Till the eyes are heavy and dim !
Seam, and gusset, and band,
   Band, and gusset, and seam,
      Till over the buttons I fall asleep.
And sew them on in a dream !

" O ! Men, with Sisters dear !
   O ! Men ! with Mothers and Wives !
It is not linen you 're wearing out,
   But human creatures' lives !
      Stitch—stitch—stitch.
   In poverty, hunger, and dirt.
Sewing at once, with a double thread.
   A Shroud as well as a Shirt.

" But why do I talk of Death ?
   That Phantom of grisly bone,
I hardly fear his terrible shape,
   It seems so like my own—

It seems so like my own,
Because of the fasts I keep,
Oh ! God ! that bread should be so dear,
And flesh and blood so cheap !

" Work—work—work !
My labour never flags ;
And what are its wages ?   A bed of straw,
A crust of bread—and rags.
That shatter'd roof—and this naked floor—
A table—a broken chair—
And a wall so blank, my shadow I thank
For sometimes falling there !

" Work—work—work !
From weary chime to chime,
Work—work—work—
As prisoners work for crime !
Band, and gusset, and seam,
Seam, and gusset, and band,
Till the heart is sick, and the brain benumb'd,
As well as the weary hand.

" Work—work—work,
In the dull December light,
  And work—work—work,
When the weather is warm and bright—
While underneath the eaves
  The brooding swallows cling
As if to show me their sunny backs
  And twit me with the spring.

  " Oh! but to breathe the breath
Of the cowslip and primrose sweet—
  With the sky above my head,
And the grass beneath my feet,
For only one short hour
  To feel as I used to feel,
Before I knew the woes of want
  And the walk that costs a meal!

" Oh but for one short hour!
  A respite however brief!
No blessed leisure for Love or Hope,
  But only time for Grief!

A little weeping would ease my heart,
　　But in their briny bed
My tears must stop, for every drop
　　Hinders needle and thread ! ''

With fingers weary and worn,
　　With eyelids heavy and red,
A Woman sate in unwomanly rags,
　　Plying her needle and thread—
　　　　Stitch ! stitch ! stitch !
　　In poverty, hunger, and dirt,
And still with a voice of dolorous pitch.
Would that its tone could reach the Rich !
　　She sang this " Song of the Shirt ! ''

THE LADY'S DREAM.

THE lady lay in her bed,
   Her couch so warm and soft,
But her sleep was restless and broken still;
   For turning often and oft
From side to side, she mutter'd and moan'd,
   And toss'd her arms aloft.

At last she startled up,
   And gaz'd on the vacant air,
With a look of awe, as if she saw
   Some dreadful phantom there—
And then in the pillow she buried her face
   From visions ill to bear.

The very curtain shook,
    Her terror was so extreme ;
And the light that fell on the broider'd quilt
    Kept a tremulous gleam :
And her voice was hollow, and shook as she cried :—
    " Oh me ! that awful dream !

" That weary, weary walk,
    In the churchyard's dismal ground !
And those horrible things, with shady wings,
    That came and flitted round,—
Death, death, and nothing but death,
    In every sight and sound !

" And oh ! those maidens young,
    Who wrought in that dreary room,
With figures drooping and spectres thin,
    And cheeks without a bloom ;—
And the Voice that cried, ' For the pomp of pride,
    We haste to an early tomb !

" · For the pomp and pleasure of Pride,

    We toil like Afric slaves,

And only to earn a home at last,

    Where yonder cypress waves;'—

And then they pointed—I never saw

    A ground so full of graves !

" And still the coffins came,

    With their sorrowful trains and slow;

Coffin after coffin still,

    A sad and sickening show;

From grief exempt, I never had dreamt

    Of such a World of Woe !

" Of the hearts that daily break,

    Of the tears that hourly fall,

Of the many, many troubles of life,

    That grieve this earthly ball—

Disease and Hunger, and Pain, and Want,

    But now I dreamt of them all !

" For the blind and the cripple were there,

 And the babe that pined for bread,

And the houseless man, and the widow poor

 Who begged—to bury the dead ;

The naked, alas, that I might have clad,

 The famish'd I might have fed !

" The sorrow I might have soothed,

 And the unregarded tears ;

For many a thronging shape was there,

 From long forgotten years,

Ay, even the poor rejected Moor,

 Who rais'd my childish fears !

" Each pleading look, that long ago

 I scann'd with a heedless eye,

Each face was gazing as plainly there,

 As when I pass'd it by :

Woe, woe for me if the past should be

 Thus present when I die !

" No need of sulphureous lake,

  No need of fiery coal,

But only that crowd of human kind

  Who wanted pity and dole—

In everlasting retrospect—

  Will wring my sinful soul !

" Alas ! I have walk'd through life

  Too heedless where I trod ;

Nay, helping to trample my fellow worm,

  And fill the burial sod—

Forgetting that even the sparrow falls

  Not unmark'd of God !

" I drank the richest draughts ;

  And ate whatever is good—

Fish, and flesh, and fowl, and fruit,

  Supplied my hungry mood ;

But I never remember'd the wretched ones

  That starve for want of food !

" I dress'd as the noble dress,
  In cloth of silver and gold,
With silk, and satin, and costly furs,
  In many an ample fold ;
But I never remember'd the naked limbs
  That froze with winter's cold.

" The wounds I might have heal'd !
  The human sorrow and smart !
And yet it never was in my soul
  To play so ill a part :
But evil is wrought by want of Thought,
  As well as want of Heart !"

She clasp'd her fervent hands,
  And the tears began to stream ;
Large, and bitter, and fast they fell,
  Remorse was so extreme ;
And yet, oh yet, that many a Dame
  Would dream the Lady's Dream !

THE WORKHOUSE CLOCK.

AN ALLEGORY.

THERE 's a murmur in the air,
And noise in every street—
The murmur of many tongues,
The noise of numerous feet—
While round the Workhouse door
The Labouring Classes flock,
For why? the Overseer of the Poor
Is setting the Workhouse Clock.

Who does not hear the tramp
Of thousands speeding along
Of either sex and various stamp,
Sickly, crippled, or strong,

Walking, limping, creeping

From court, and alley, and lane,

But all in one direction sweeping

Like rivers that seek the main ?

Who does not see them sally

From mill, and garret, and room,

In lane, and court and alley,

From homes in poverty's lowest valley,

Furnished with shuttle and loom—

Poor slaves of Civilization's galley—

And in the road and footways rally,

As if for the Day of Doom ?

Some, of hardly human form,

Stunted, crooked, and crippled by toil ;

Dingy with smoke and dust and oil,

And smirch'd besides with vicious soil,

Clustering, mustering, all in a swarm.

Father, mother, and careful child,

Looking as if it had never smiled—

The Sempstress, lean, and weary, and wan,

With only the ghosts of garments on—

The Weaver, her sallow neighbour,

The grim and sooty Artisan ;
Every soul—child, woman, or man,
Who lives—or dies—by labour.

Stirred by an overwhelming zeal,
And social impulse, a terrible throng !
Leaving shuttle, and needle, and wheel,
Furnace, and grindstone, spindle, and reel,
Thread, and yarn, and iron, and steel—
Yea, rest and the yet untasted meal—
Gushing, rushing, crushing along,
A very torrent of Man !
Urged by the sighs of sorrow and wrong,
Grown at last to a hurricane strong,
Stop its course who can !
Stop who can its onward course
And irresistible moral force ;
O ! vain and idle dream !
For surely as men are all akin,
Whether of fair or sable skin,
According to Nature's scheme,

That Human Movement contains within
A Blood-Power stronger than Steam.

Onward, onward, with hasty feet,
They swarm—and westward still—
Masses born to drink and eat,
But starving amidst Whitechapel's meat,
And famishing down Cornhill !
Through the Poultry—but still unfed—
Christian Charity, hang your head !
Hungry—passing the Street of Bread ;
Thirsty—the Street of Milk ;
Ragged—beside the Ludgate Mart,
So gorgeous, through Mechanic-Art,
With cotton, and wool, and silk !

At last, before that door
That bears so many a knock
Ere ever it opens to Sick or Poor,
Like sheep they huddle and flock—
And would that all the Good and Wise
Could see the Million of hollow eyes,

With a gleam deriv'd from Hope and the skies.
Upturn'd to the Workhouse Clock!

Oh! that the Parish Powers,
Who regulate Labour's hours,
The daily amount of human trial,
Weariness, pain, and self-denial
Would turn from the artificial dial
That striketh ten or eleven,
And go, for once, by that older one
That stands in the light of Nature's sun
And takes its time from Heaven!

My DEAR SIR,—The following Ode was written anticipating the tone of some strictures on my writings, by the gentleman to whom it is addressed. I have not seen his book ; but I know by hearsay that some of my verses are characterised as " profaneness and ribaldry "—citing, in proof, the description of a certain sow, from whose jaw a cabbage sprout—

> Protruded, as the dove so staunch
> For peace supports an olive branch.

If the printed works of my Censor had not prepared me for any misapplication of *types*, I should have been surprised by this misapprehension of one of the commonest emblems. In some cases the dove unquestionably stands for the Divine Spirit ; but the same bird is also a lay representative of the peace of this world, and, as such, has figured time out of mind in allegorical pictures. The sense in which it was used by me is plain from the context ; at least, it would be plain to any one but a fisher for faults, predisposed to carp at some things, to dab at others, and to flounder in all. But I am possibly in error. It is the female swine, perhaps, that is profaned in the eyes of the Oriental tourist. Men find strange ways of marking their intolerance ; and the spirit is certainly strong enough, in Mr. W.'s works, to set up a creature as sacred, in sheer opposition to the Mussulman, with whom she is a beast of abomination. It would only be going the whole sow.

I am, dear Sir, yours very truly,

THOS. HOOD.

1837.

ODE TO RAE WILSON, ESQUIRE.

Close, close your eyes with holy dread,
And weave a circle round him thrice;
For he on honey-dew hath fed,
And drunk the milk of Paradise!
                              COLERIDGE.

It's very hard them kind of men
Won't let a body be.
                              OLD BALLAD.

A WANDERER, Wilson, from my native land,

Remote, O Rae, from godliness and thee,

Where rolls between us the eternal sea,

Besides some furlongs of a foreign sand,—

Beyond the broadest Scotch of London Wall;

Beyond the loudest Saint that has a call;

Across the wavy waste between us stretch'd,

A friendly missive warns me of a stricture,

Wherein my likeness you have darkly etch'd,

And tho' I have not seen the shadow sketch'd,

Thus I remark prophetic on the picture.

I guess the features:—in a line to paint
Their moral ugliness, I 'm not a saint.
Not one of those self-constituted saints,
Quacks—not physicians—in the cure of souls,
Censors who sniff out mortal taints,
And call the devil over his own coals—
Those pseudo Privy Councillors of God,
Who write down judgments with a pen hard-nibb'd ;
    Ushers of Beelzebub's Black Rod,
Commending sinners, not to ice thick-ribb'd,
But endless flames, to scorch them up like flax,—
Yet sure of heav'n themselves, as if they'd cribb'd
Th' impression of St. Peter's keys in wax !

Of such a character no single trace
Exists, I know, in my fictitious face ;
There wants a certain cast about the eye ;
A certain lifting of the nose's tip ;
A certain curling of the nether lip,
In scorn of all that is, beneath the sky ;
In brief it is an aspect deleterious,
A face decidedly not serious,

A face profane, that would not do at all
To make a face at Exeter Hall,—
That Hall where bigots rant, and cant, and pray,
And laud each other face to face,
Till ev'ry farthing-candle *ray*
Conceives itself a great gas-light of grace !

Well !—be the graceless lineaments confest !
I do enjoy this bounteous beauteous earth ;
 And dote upon a jest
" Within the limits of becoming mirth ; "—
No solemn sanctimonious face I pull,
Nor think I 'm pious when I 'm only bilious—
Nor study in my sanctum supercilious
To frame a Sabbath Bill or forge a Bull.
I pray for grace—repent each sinful act—
Peruse, but underneath the rose, my Bible ;
And love my neighbour, far too well, in fact,
To call and twit him with a godly tract
That 's turn'd by application to a libel.
My heart ferments not with the bigot's leaven,
All creeds I view with toleration thorough,

And have a horror of regarding heaven
    As anybody's rotten borough.

What else ? no part I take in party fray,
With tropes from Billingsgate's slang-whanging tartars,
I fear no Pope—and let great Ernest play
At Fox and Goose with Fox's Martyrs !
1 own I laugh at over-righteous men,
I own 1 shake my sides at ranters,
And treat sham-Abr'am saints with wicked banters,
I even own, that there are times—but then
It 's when I 've got my wine—I say d——canters !

I 've no ambition to enact the spy
On fellow souls, a Spiritual Pry—
'Tis said that people ought to guard their noses
Who thrust them into matters none of theirs ;
And, tho' no delicacy discomposes
Your Saint, yet I consider faith and pray'rs
Amongst the privatest of men's affairs.

I do not hash the Gospel in my books,
And thus upon the public mind intrude it,

As if I thought, like Otaheitan cooks,
No food was fit to eat till I had chew'd it.
On Bible stilts I don't affect to stalk;
Nor lard with Scripture my familiar talk,—
　　For man may pious texts repeat,
And yet religion have no inward seat;
'Tis not so plain as the old Hill of Howth,
A man has got his belly full of meat
Because he talks with victuals in his mouth !

Mere verbiage,—it is not worth a carrot !
Why, Socrates or Plato—where 's the odds ?—
Once taught a jay to supplicate the Gods,
And made a Polly-theist of a Parrot !

A mere professor, spite of all his cant, is
　　Not a whit better than a Mantis,—
An insect, of what clime I can't determine,
That lifts its paws most parson-like, and thence,
By simple savages—thro' sheer pretence—
Is reckon'd quite a saint amongst the vermin.

But where 's the reverence, or where the *nous*,

To ride on one's religion thro' the lobby,

    Whether as stalking-horse or hobby,

To show its pious paces to " the House "?

I honestly confess that I would hinder

The Scottish member's legislative rigs,

    That spiritual Pinder,

Who looks on erring souls as straying pigs,

That must be lash'd by law, wherever found,

And driv'n to church as to the parish pound.

' I do confess, without reserve or wheedle,

I view that grovelling idea as one

· Worthy some parish clerk's ambitious son,

A charity-boy who longs to be a beadle.

On such a vital topic sure 'tis odd

How much a man can differ from his neighbour :

One wishes worship freely giv'n to God,

Another wants to make it statute-labour—

The broad distinction in a line to draw,

As means to lead us to the skies above,

You say—Sir Andrew and his love of law,
And I—the Saviour with his law of love.

Spontaneously to God should tend the soul,
Like the magnetic needle to the Pole;
But what were that intrinsic virtue worth,
Suppose some fellow, with more zeal than knowledge,
 Fresh from St. Andrew's College,
Should nail the conscious needle to the north?

I do confess that I abhor and shrink
From schemes, with a religious willy-nilly,
That frown upon St. Giles's sins, but blink
The peccadilloes of all Piccadilly—
My soul revolts at such bare hypocrisy,
And will not, dare not, fancy in accord
The Lord of Hosts with an Exclusive Lord
 Of this world's aristocracy.
It will not own a notion so unholy,
As thinking that the rich by easy trips
May go to heav'n, whereas the poor and lowly
Must work their passage, as they do in ships.

One place there is—beneath the burial sod
Where all mankind are equalised by death ;
Another place there is—the Fane of God,
Where all are equal who draw living breath ;—
Juggle who will *elsewhere* with his own soul,
Playing the Judas with a temporal dole—
He who can come beneath that awful cope,
In the dread presence of a Maker just,
Who metes to ev'ry pinch of human dust
One even measure of immortal hope—
He who can stand within that holy door,
With soul unbow'd by that pure spirit-level,
And frame unequal laws for rich and poor,—
Might sit for Hell and represent the Devil !

Such are the solemn sentiments, O Rae,
In your last Journey-Work, perchance, you ravage,
Seeming, but in more courtly terms, to say
I 'm but a heedless, creedless, godless, savage ;
A very Guy, deserving fire and faggots,—
　　A Scoffer, always on the grin,

And sadly given to the mortal sin
Of liking Mawworms less than merry maggots !

The humble records of my life to search,
I have not herded with mere pagan beasts ;
But sometimes I have " sat at good men's feasts,"
And I have been "where bells have knoll'd to church."
Dear bells ! how sweet the sounds of village bells
When on the undulating air they swim !
Now loud as welcomes ! faint, now, as farewells !
And trembling all about the breezy dells,
As flutter'd by the wings of Cherubim.
Meanwhile the bees are chaunting a low hymn ;
And lost to sight th' extatic lark above
Sings, like a soul beatified, of love,—
With, now and then, the coo of the wild pigeon ;—
O Pagans, Heathens, Infidels, and Doubters !
If such sweet sounds can't woo you to religion,
Will the harsh voices of church cads and touters ?

A man may cry Church ! Church ! at ev'ry word,
With no more piety than other people—

A daw 's not reckon'd a religious bird
Because it keeps a-cawing from a steeple.
The Temple is a good, a holy place,
But quacking only gives it an ill savour;
While saintly mountebanks the porch disgrace,
And bring religion's self into disfavour!

Behold yon servitor of God and Mammon,
Who, binding up his Bible with his Ledger,
    Blends Gospel texts with trading gammon,
A black-leg saint, a spiritual hedger,
Who backs his rigid Sabbath, so to speak,
Against the wicked remnant of the week,
A saving bet against his sinful bias—
" Rogue that I am," he whispers to himself,
" I lie—I cheat—do anything for pelf,
But who on earth can say I am not pious?"

In proof how over-righteousness re-acts,
Accept an anecdote well bas'd on facts.

One Sunday morning—(at the day don't fret)—
In riding with a friend to Ponder's End
Outside the stage, we happen'd to commend
A certain mansion that we saw To Let.
" Ay," cried our coachman, with our talk to grapple.
" You 're right! no house along the road comes nigh it !
'Twas built by the same man as built yon chapel.

 And master wanted once to buy it,—
But t'other driv the bargain much too hard—
 He ax'd sure-*ly* a sum purdigious !
But being so particular religious,
Why, *that,* you see, put master on his guard ! "

 Church is " a little heav'n below,
 I have been there and still would go,"—
Yet I am none of those who think it odd
 A man can pray unbidden from the cassock,
 And, passing by the customary hassock,
Kneel down remote upon the simple sod,
And sue in formâ pauperis to God.

As for the rest,—intolerant to none,
Whatever shape the pious rite may bear,

Ev'n the poor Pagan's homage to the Sun
I would not harshly scorn, lest even there
I spurn'd some elements of Christian pray'r—
An aim, tho' erring, at a " world ayont "—
Acknowledgment of good—of man's futility,
A sense of need, and weakness, and indeed
That very thing so many Christians want—
        Humility.

Such, unto Papists, Jews, or turban'd Turks,
Such is my spirit—(I don't mean my wraith !)
Such, may it please you, is my humble faith ;
I know, full well, you do not like my *works !*

I have not sought, 'tis true, the Holy Land,
As full of texts as Cuddie Headrigg's mother,
        The Bible in one hand,
And my own common-place-book in the other—
But you have been to Palestine—alas !
Some minds improve by travel, others, rather,
        Resemble copper wire, or brass,
Which gets the narrower by going farther !

Worthless are all such Pilgrimages—very!
If Palmers at the Holy Tomb contrive
The human heats and rancour to revive
That at the Sepulchre they ought to bury.
A sorry sight it is to rest the eye on,
To see a Christian creature graze at Sion,
Then homeward, of the saintly pasture full,
Rush bellowing, and breathing fire and smoke,
At crippled Papistry to butt and poke,
Exactly as a skittish Scottish bull
Hunts an old woman in a scarlet cloke?

Why leave a serious, moral, pious home,
Scotland, renown'd for sanctity of old,
Far distant Catholics to rate and scold
For—doing as the Romans do at Rome?
With such a bristling spirit wherefore quit
The Land of Cakes for any land of wafers,
About the graceless images to flit,
And buzz and chafe importunate as chafers,
Longing to carve the carvers to Scotch collops—?
People who hold such absolute opinions

Should stay at home, in Protestant dominions,
  Not travel like male Mrs. Trollopes.

  Gifted with noble tendency to climb,
    Yet weak at the same time,
Faith is a kind of parasitic plant,
That grasps the nearest stem with tendril-rings ;
And as the climate and the soil may grant,
So is the sort of tree to which it clings.
Consider, then, before, like Hurlothrumbo,
You aim your club at any creed on earth,
That, by the simple accident of birth,
You might have been High Priest to Mumbo Jumbo.

For me—thro' heathen ignorance perchance,
Not having knelt in Palestine,—I feel
None of that griffinish excess of zeal,
Some travellers would blaze with here in France
Dolls I can see in Virgin-like array,
Nor for a scuffle with the idols hanker
Like crazy Quixotte at the puppet's play,
If their " offence be rank," should mine be *rancour ?*

Mild light, and by degrees, should be the plan
To cure the dark and erring mind ;
But who would rush at a benighted man,
And give him two black eyes for being blind ?

Suppose the tender but luxuriant hop
Around a canker'd stem should twine,
What Kentish boor would tear away the prop
So roughly as to wound, nay kill the bine ?

The images, 'tis true, are strangely dress'd,
With gauds and toys extremely out of season :
The carving nothing of the very best,
The whole repugnant to the eye of reason,
Shocking to Taste, and to Fine Arts a treason—
Yet ne'er o'erlook in bigotry of sect
One truly *Catholic*, one common form,
      At which uncheck'd
All Christian hearts may kindle or keep warm.

Say, was it to my spirit's gain or loss,
One bright and balmy morning, as I went

From Liege's lovely environs to Ghent,

If hard by the wayside I found a cross,

That made me breathe a pray'r upon the spot—

While Nature of herself, as if to trace

The emblem's use, had trail'd around its base

The blue significant Forget-Me-Not ?

Methought, the claims of charity to urge

More forcibly, along with Faith and Hope,

The pious choice had pitch'd upon the verge

    Of a delicious slope,

Giving the eye much variegated scope ;—

" Look round," it whisper'd, " on that prospect rare,

Those vales so verdant, and those hills so blue ;

Enjoy the sunny world, so fresh, and fair,

But "—(how the simple legend pierc'd me thro' !)

    " Priez pour les Malheureux."

With sweet kind natures, as in honey'd cells,

Religion lives, and feels herself at home ;

But only on a formal visit dwells

Where wasps instead of bees have form'd the comb.

Shun pride, O Rae !—whatever sort beside
You take in lieu, shun spiritual pride !
A pride there is of rank—a pride of birth,
A pride of learning, and a pride of purse,
A London pride—in short, there be on earth
A host of prides, some better and some worse ;
But of all prides, since Lucifer's attaint,
The proudest swells a self-elected Saint.

To picture that cold pride so harsh and hard,
Fancy a peacock in a poultry yard.
Behold him in conceited circles sail,
Strutting and dancing, and now planted stiff,
In all his pomp of pageantry, as if
He felt "the eyes of Europe" on his tail !
As for the humble breed retain'd by man,
    He scorns the whole domestic clan—
    He bows, he bridles,
    He wheels, he sidles,
At last, with stately dodgings, in a corner
He pens a simple russet hen, to scorn her
Full in the blaze of his resplendent fan !

" Look here," he cries, (to give him words,)
    " Thou feather'd clay,—thou scum of birds !''
Flirting the rustling plumage in her eyes,—
" Look here, thou vile predestin'd sinner,
    Doom'd to be roasted for a dinner,
Behold these lovely variegated dyes !
These are the rainbow colours of the skies,
That heav'n has shed upon me *con amore*—
A Bird of Paradise ?—a pretty story !
I am that Saintly Fowl, thou paltry chick !
    Look at my crown of glory !
Thou dingy, dirty, dabbled, draggled jill !''
And off goes Partlet, wriggling from a kick,
With bleeding scalp laid open by his bill !

That little simile exactly paints
How sinners are despis'd by saints.
By saints !—the Hypocrites that ope heav'n's door
Obsequious to the sinful man of riches—
But put the wicked, naked, barelegg'd poor,
    In parish stocks instead of breeches.

The Saints!—the Bigots that in public spout,
Spread phosphorus of zeal on scraps of fustian,
And go like walking " Lucifers " about
    Mere living bundles of combustion.

The Saints!—the aping Fanatics that talk
All cant and rant and rhapsodies highflown—
    That bid you baulk
    A Sunday walk,
And shun God's work as you should shun your own.

The Saints!—the Formalists, the extra pious,
Who think the mortal husk can save the soul,
By trundling, with a mere mechanic bias,
To church, just like a lignum-vitæ bowl!
         .

The Saints!—the Pharisees, whose beadle stands
    Beside a stern coercive kirk,
    A piece of human mason-work,
Calling all sermons contrabands,
In that great Temple that 's not made with hands!

Thrice blessed, rather, is the man with whom
The gracious prodigality of nature,
The balm, the bliss, the beauty, and the bloom,
The bounteous providence in ev'ry feature,
Recall the good Creator to his creature,
Making all earth a fane, all heav'n its dome!
To *his* tun'd spirit the wild heather-bells
  Ring Sabbath knells;
The jubilate of the soaring lark
  Is chaunt of clerk;
For Choir, the thrush and the gregarious linnet;
The sod 's a cushion for his pious want;
And, consecrated by the heav'n within it
  The sky-blue pool, a font.
Each cloud-capp'd mountain is a holy altar;
  An organ breathes in every grove;
  And the full heart 's a Psalter,
Rich in deep hymns of gratitude and love!

Sufficiently by-stern necessitarians
Poor Nature, with her face begrim'd by dust,

Is stok'd, cok'd, smok'd, and almost chok'd; but must

Religion have its own Utilitarians,

Labell'd with evangelical phylacteries,

To make the road to heav'n a railway trust,

And churches—that 's the naked fact—mere factories ?

Oh ! simply open wide the Temple door,

And let the solemn, swelling, organ greet,

 With *Voluntaries* meet,

The *willing* advent of the rich and poor !

And while to God the loud Hosannas soar,

With rich vibrations from the vocal throng—

From quiet shades that to the woods belong,

 And brooks with music of their own,

Voices may come to swell the choral song

With notes of praise they learn'd in musings lone.

How strange it is while on all vital questions,

That occupy the House and public mind,

We always meet with some humane suggestions

Of gentle measures of a healing kind,

Instead of harsh severity and vigour,

The Saint alone his preference retains
      For bills of penalties and pains,
And marks his narrow code with legal rigour !
Why shun, as worthless of affiliation,
What men of all political persuasion
Extol—and even use upon occasion—
That Christian principle, conciliation ?
But possibly the men who make such fuss
With Sunday pippins and old Trots infirm,
Attach some other meaning to the term,
                  As thus :

One market morning, in my usual rambles,
Passing along Whitechapel's ancient shambles,
Where meat was hung in many a joint and quarter.
I had to halt awhile, like other folks,
            To let a killing butcher coax
A score of lambs and fatted sheep to slaughter.
A sturdy man he look'd to fell an ox,
Bull-fronted, ruddy, with a formal streak
Of well-greas'd hair down either cheek,

As if he dee-dash-dee'd some other flocks
Besides those woolly-headed stubborn blocks
That stood before him, in vexatious huddle—
Poor little lambs, with bleating wethers group'd,
While, now and then, a thirsty creature stoop'd
And meekly snuff'd, but did not taste the puddle.

Fierce bark'd the dog, and many a blow was dealt,
That loin, and chump, and scrag and saddle felt,
Yet still, that fatal step they all declin'd it,—
And shunn'd the tainted door as if they smelt
Onions, mint sauce, and lemon juice behind it.
At last there came a pause of brutal force,
    The cur was silent, for his jaws were full
    Of tangled locks of tarry wool,
The man had whoop'd and bellow'd till dead hoarse,
The time was ripe for mild expostulation,
And thus it stammer'd from a stander-by—
"Zounds!—my good fellow,—it quite makes me—why
It really—my dear fellow—do just try
      Conciliation!"

Stringing his nerves like flint,
The sturdy butcher seiz'd upon the hint,—
At least he seiz'd upon the foremost wether,—
And hugg'd and lugg'd and tugg'd him neck and crop
Just *nolens volens* thro' the open shop—
If tails come off he didn't care a feather,—
Then walking to the door, and smiling grim,
He rubb'd his forehead and his sleeve together—
    " There !—I've *conciliated* him !"

Again—good-humouredly to end our quarrel—
    (Good humour should prevail !)
    I 'll fit you with a tale
    Whereto is tied a moral.

Once on a time a certain English lass
Was seiz'd with symptoms of such deep decline,
Cough, hectic flushes, ev'ry evil sign,
That, as their wont is at such desperate pass,
The Doctors gave her over—to an ass.

Accordingly, the grisly Shade to bilk,

Each morn the patient quaff'd a frothy bowl

    Of asinine new milk,

Robbing a shaggy suckling of a foal

Which got proportionably spare and skinny—

Meanwhile the neighbours cried " poor Mary Ann !

She can't get over it ! she never can !"

When lo ! to prove each prophet was a ninny

The one that died was the poor wetnurse Jenny.

    To aggravate the case,

There were but two grown donkeys in the place ;

And most unluckily for Eve's sick daughter,

The other long-ear'd creature was a male,

Who never in his life had given a pail

    Of milk, or even chalk and water.

No matter : at the usual hour of eight

Down trots a donkey to the wicket-gate,

With Mister Simon Gubbins on his back,—

" Your sarvant, Miss,—a werry spring-like day,—

Bad time for hasses tho' ! good lack ! good lack !

Jenny be dead, Miss,—but I'ze brought ye Jack,
He doesn't give no milk—but he can bray."

      So runs the story,
And, in vain self-glory,
Some Saints would sneer at Gubbins for his blindness—
But what the better are their pious saws
To ailing souls, than dry hee-haws,
Without the milk of human kindness ?

THE TWO SWANS.

A FAIRY TALE.

.

I.

IMMORTAL Imogen, crown'd queen above

The lilies of thy sex, vouchsafe to hear

A fairy dream in honour of true love—

True above ills, and frailty, and all fear—

Perchance a shadow of his own career

Whose youth was darkly prison'd and long twined

By serpent-sorrow, till white Love drew near,

And sweetly sang him free, and round his mind

A bright horizon threw, wherein no grief may wind.

II.

I saw a tower builded on a lake,
Mock'd by its inverse shadow, dark and deep—
That seem'd a still intenser night to make,
Wherein the quiet waters sunk to sleep,—
And, whatsoe'er was prison'd in that keep,
A monstrous Snake was warden :—round and round
In sable ringlets I beheld him creep
Blackest amid black shadows to the ground,
Whilst his enormous head the topmost turret crown'd.

III.

From whence he shot fierce light against the stars,
Making the pale moon paler with affright ;
And with his ruby eye out-threaten'd Mars—
That blazed in the mid-heavens, hot and bright—
Nor slept, nor wink'd, but with a steadfast spite
Watch'd their wan looks and tremblings in the skies ;
And that he might not slumber in the night,
The curtain-lids were pluck'd from his large eyes,
So he might never drowse, but watch his secret prize.

IV.

Prince or princess in dismal durance pent,

Victims of old Enchantment's love or hate,

Their lives must all in painful sighs be spent,

Watching the lonely waters soon and late,

And clouds that pass and leave them to their fate,

Or company their grief with heavy tears :—

Meanwhile that Hope can spy no golden gate

For sweet escapement, but in darksome fears

They weep and pine away as if immortal years.

V.

No gentle bird with gold upon its wing

Will perch upon the grate—the gentle bird

Is safe in leafy dell, and will not bring

Freedom's sweet key-note and commission word

Learn'd of a fairy's lips, for pity stirr'd—

Lest while he trembling sings, untimely guest !

Watch'd by that cruel Snake and darkly heard,

He leave a widow on her lonely nest,

To press in silent grief the darlings of her breast.

VI.

No gallant knight, adventurous, in his bark,
Will seek the fruitful perils of the place,
To rouse with dipping oar the waters dark
That bear that serpent-image on their face.
And Love, brave Love ! though he attempt the base,
Nerved to his loyal death, he may not win
His captive lady from the strict embrace
Of that foul Serpent, clasping her within
His sable folds—like Eve enthrall'd by the old Sin.

VII.

But there is none—no knight in panoply,
Nor Love, intrench'd in his strong steely coat :
No little speck—no sail—no helper nigh,
No sign—no whispering—no plash of boat :—
The distant shores show dimly and remote,
Made of a deeper mist,—serene and grey,—
And slow and mute the cloudy shadows float
Over the gloomy wave, and pass away,
Chased by the silver beams that on their marges play.

VIII.

And bright and silvery the willows sleep
Over the shady verge—no mad winds tease
Their hoary heads ; but quietly they weep
There sprinkling leaves—half fountains and half trees :
There lilies be—and fairer than all these,
A solitary Swan her breast of snow
Launches against the wave that seems to freeze
Into a chaste reflection, still below
Twin-shadow of herself wherever she may go.

IX.

And forth she paddles in the very noon
Of solemn midnight like an elfin thing,
Charm'd into being by the argent moon—
Whose silver light for love of her fair wing
Goes with her in the shade, still worshipping
Her dainty plumage :—all around her grew
A radiant circlet, like a fairy ring ;
And all behind, a tiny little clue
Of light, to guide her back across the waters blue.

X.

And sure she is no meaner than a fay,
Redeem'd from sleepy death, for beauty's sake,
By old ordainment :—silent as she lay,
Touch'd by a moonlight wand I saw her wake,
And cut her leafy slough, and so forsake
The verdant prison of her lily peers,
That slept amidst the stars upon the lake—
A breathing shape—restored to human fears,
And new-born love and grief—self-conscious of her tears.

XI.

And now she clasps her wings around her heart,
And near that lonely isle begins to glide
Pale as her fears, and oft-times with a start
Turns her impatient head from side to side
In universal terrors—all too wide
To watch ; and often to that marble keep
Upturns her pearly eyes, as if she spied
Some foe, and crouches in the shadow's steep
That in the gloomy wave go diving fathoms deep.

XII.

And well she may, to spy that fearful thing

All down the dusky walls in circlets wound ;

Alas ! for what rare prize, with many a ring

Girding the marble casket round and round ?

His folded tail, lost in the gloom profound,

Terribly darkeneth the rocky base ;

But on the top his monstrous head is crown'd

With prickly spears, and on his doubtful face

Gleam his unwearied eyes, red watchers of the place.

XIII.

Alas ! of the hot fires that nightly fall,

No one will scorch him in those orbs of spite,

So he may never see beneath the wall

That timid little creature, all too bright,

That stretches her fair neck, slender and white,

Invoking the pale moon, and vainly tries

Her throbbing throat, as if to charm the night

With song—but, hush—it perishes in sighs,

And there will be no dirge sad-swelling though she dies !

XIV.

She droops—she sinks—she leans upon the lake,

Fainting again into a lifeless flower;

But soon the chilly springs anoint and wake

Her spirit from its death, and with new power

She sheds her stifled sorrows in a shower

Of tender song, timed to her falling tears—

That wins the shady summit of that tower,

And, trembling all the sweeter for its fears,

Fills with imploring moan that cruel monster's ears.

XV.

And, lo ! the scaly beast is all deprest,

Subdued like Argus by the might of sound—

What time Apollo his sweet lute addrest

To magic converse with the air, and bound

The many monster eyes, all slumber-drown'd :—

So on the turret-top that watchful Snake

Pillows his giant head, and lists profound,

As if his wrathful spite would never wake,

Charm'd into sudden sleep for Love and Beauty's sake !

XVI.

His prickly crest lies prone upon his crown,

And thirsty lip from lip disparted flies,

To drink that dainty flood of music down—

His scaly throat is big with pent-up sighs—

And whilst his hollow car entrancèd lies,

His looks for envy of the charmed sense

Are fain to listen, till his steadfast eyes,

Stung into pain by their own impotence,

Distil enormous tears into the lake immense.

XVII.

Oh, tuneful Swan! oh, melancholy bird!

Sweet was that midnight miracle of song,

Rich with ripe sorrow, needful of no word

To tell of pain, and love, and love's deep wrong—

Hinting a piteous tale—perchance how long

Thy unknown tears were mingled with the lake,

What time disguised thy leafy mates among—

And no eye knew what human love and ache

Dwelt in those dewy leaves, and heart so nigh to break.

XVIII.

Therefore no poet will ungently touch
The water-lily, on whose eyelids dew
Trembles like tears ; but ever hold it such
As human pain may wander through and through,
Turning the pale leaf paler in its hue—
Wherein life dwells, transfigured, not entomb'd,
By magic spells.   Alas ! who ever knew
Sorrow in all its shapes, leafy and plumed,
Or in gross husks of brutes eternally inhumed ?

XIX.

And now the wingèd song has scaled the height
Of that dark dwelling, builded for despair,
And soon a little casement flashing bright
Widens self-open'd into the cool air—
That music like a bird may enter there
And soothe the captive in his stony cage ;
For there is nought of grief, or painful care,
But plaintive song may happily engage
From sense of its own ill, and tenderly assuage.

XX.

And forth into the light, small and remote,

A creature, like the fair son of a king,

Draws to the lattice in his jewell'd coat

Against the silver moonlight glistening,

And leans upon his white hand listening

To that sweet music that with tenderer tone

Salutes him, wondering what kindly thing

Is come to soothe him with so tuneful moan,

Singing beneath the walls as if for him alone !

XXI.

And while he listens, the mysterious song,

Woven with timid particles of speech,

Twines into passionate words that grieve along

The melancholy notes, and softly teach

The secrets of true love,—that trembling reach

His earnest ear, and through the shadows dun

He missions like replies, and each to each

Their silver voices mingle into one,

Like blended streams that make one music as they run.

XXII.

" Ah ! Love, my hope is swooning in my heart,—

Ay, sweet, my cage is strong and hung full high—

Alas ! our lips are held so far apart,

Thy words come faint, they have so far to fly !—

If I may only shun that serpent-eye,—

Ah, me ! that serpent-eye doth never sleep ;—

Then, nearer thee, Love's martyr, I will die !—

Alas, alas ! that word has made me weep !

For pity's sake remain safe in thy marble keep !

XXIII.

My marble keep ! it is my marble tomb—

Nay, sweet ! but thou hast there thy living breath—

Aye to expend in sighs for this hard doom ;—

But I will come to thee and sing beneath,

And nightly so beguile this serpent wreath ;—

Nay, I will find a path from these despairs.

Ah, needs then thou must tread the back of death,

Making his stony ribs thy stony stairs.—

Behold his ruby eye, how fearfully it glares !"

XXIV.

Full sudden at these words, the princely youth
Leaps on the scaly back that slumbers, still
Unconscious of his foot, yet not for ruth,
But numb'd to dulness by the fairy skill
Of that sweet music (all more wild and shrill
For intense fear) that charm'd him as he lay--
Meanwhile the lover nerves his desperate will,
Held some short throbs by natural dismay,
Then down, down the serpent-track begins his darksome
way.

XXV.

Now dimly seen—now toiling out of sight,
Eclipsed and cover'd by the envious wall ;
Now fair and spangled in the sudden light,
And clinging with wide arms for fear of fall ;
Now dark and shelter'd by a kindly pall
Of dusky shadow from his wakeful foe :
Slowly he winds adown—dimly and small,
Watch'd by the gentle Swan that sings below,
Her hope increasing, still, the larger he doth grow.

XXVI.

But nine times nine the serpent folds embrace
The marble walls about—which he must tread
Before his anxious foot may touch the base :
Long is the dreary path, and must be sped !
But Love, that holds the mastery of dread,
Braces his spirit, and with constant toil
He wins his way, and now, with arms outspread,
Impatient plunges from the last long coil :
So may all gentle Love ungentle Malice foil.

XXVII.

The song is hush'd, the charm is all complete,
And two fair Swans are swimming on the lake :
But scarce their tender bills have time to meet,
When fiercely drops adown that cruel Snake—
His steely scales a fearful rustling make,
Like autumn leaves that tremble and foretell
The sable storm ;—the plumy lovers quake—
And feel the troubled waters pant and swell,
Heaved by the giant bulk of their pursuer fell.

XXVIII.

His jaws, wide yawning like the gates of Death.

Hiss horrible pursuit—his red eyes glare

The waters into blood—his eager breath

Grows hot upon their plumes :—now, minstrel fair !

She drops her ring into the waves, and there

It widens all around, a fairy ring

Wrought of the silver light—the fearful pair

Swim in the very midst, and pant and cling

The closer for their fears, and tremble wing to wing.

XXIX.

Bending their course over the pale grey lake,

Against the pallid East, wherein light play'd

In tender flushes, still the baffled Snake

Circled them round continually, and bay'd

Hoarsely and loud, forbidden to invade

The sanctuary ring—his sable mail

Roll'd darkly through the flood, and writhed and made

A shining track over the waters pale,

Lash'd into boiling foam by his enormous tail.

XXX.

And so they sail'd into the distance dim,

Into the very distance—small and white,

Like snowy blossoms of the spring that swim

Over the brooklets—follow'd by the spite

Of that huge Serpent, that with wild affright

Worried them on their course, and sore annoy.

Till on the grassy marge I saw them 'light,

And change, anon, a gentle girl and boy,

Lock'd in embrace of sweet unutterable joy !

XXXI.

Then came the Morn, and with her pearly showers

Wept on them, like a mother, in whose eyes

Tears are no grief ; and from his rosy bowers

The Oriental sun began to rise,

Chasing the darksome shadows from the skies :

Wherewith that sable Serpent far away

Fled, like a part of night—delicious sighs

From waking blossoms purified the day,

And little birds were singing sweetly from each spray.

ODE

ON A DISTANT PROSPECT OF CLAPHAM ACADEMY. *

Ah me ! those old familiar bounds !
That classic house, those classic grounds
  My pensive thought recalls !
What tender urchins now confine,
What little captives now repine,
  Within yon irksome walls !

Ay, that 's the very house ! I know
Its ugly windows, ten a-row !
  Its chimneys in the rear !
And there 's the iron rod so high,
That drew the thunder from the sky
  And turn'd our table-beer !

* No connexion with any other Ode.

There I was birch'd ! there I was bred !
There like a little Adam fed
   From Learning's woeful tree !
The weary tasks I used to con !—
The hopeless leaves I wept upon !—
   Most fruitless leaves to me !—

The summon'd class !—the awful bow !—
I wonder who is master now
   And wholesome anguish sheds !
How many ushers now employs,
How many maids to see the boys
   Have nothing in their heads !

And Mrs. S * * * ?—Doth she abet
(Like Pallas in the parlour) yet
   Some favour'd two or three,—
The little Crichtons of the hour,
Her muffin-medals that devour,
   And swill her prize——bohea ?

Ay, there 's the play-ground! there 's the lime,
Beneath whose shade in summer's prime
  So wildly I have read!—
Who sits there *now*, and skims the cream
Of young Romance, and weaves a dream
  Of Love and Cottage-bread?

Who struts the Randall of the walk?
Who models tiny heads in chalk?
  Who scoops the light canoe?
What early genius buds apace?
Where 's Poynter? Harris? Bowers? Chase?
  Hal Baylis? blithe Carew?

Alack! they 're gone—a thousand ways!
And some are serving in " the Greys."
  And some have perish'd young! –
Jack Harris weds his second wife;
Hal Baylis drives the wane of life;
  And blithe Carew—is hung!

Grave Bowers teaches A B C
To savages at Owhyee ;
  Poor Chase is with the worms !—
All, all are gone—the olden breed !—
New crops of mushroom boys succeed,
  " And push us from our *forms!* "

Lo ! where they scramble forth, and shout,
And leap, and skip, and mob about,
  At play where we have play'd !
Some hop, some run, (some fall,) some twine
Their crony arms ; some in the shine,
  And some are in the shade !

Lo there what mix'd conditions run !
The orphan lad ; the widow's son ;
  And Fortune's favour'd care—
The wealthy born, for whom she hath
Mac-Adamised the future path—
  The Nabob's pamper'd heir !

Some brightly starr'd—some evil born,—
For honour some, and some for scorn,—
 For fair or foul renown !
Good, bad, indiff'rent—none may lack !
Look, here's a White, and there's a Black !
 And there's a Creole brown !

Some laugh and sing, some mope and weep,
And wish *their* frugal sires would keep
 Their only sons at home ;—
Some tease the future tense, and plan
The full-grown doings of the man,
 And pant for years to come !

A foolish wish ! There's one at hoop ;
And four at *fives !* and five who stoop
 The marble taw to speed !
And one that curvets in and out,
Reining his fellow Cob about,—
 Would I were in his *steed !*

Yet he would gladly halt and drop
That boyish harness off, to swop
   With this world's heavy van—
To toil, to tug.   O little fool !
While thou canst be a horse at school
   To wish to be a man !

Perchance thou deem'st it were a thing
To wear a crown,—to be a king !
   And sleep on regal down !
Alas ! thou know'st not kingly cares ;
Far happier is thy head that wears
   That hat without a crown !

And dost thou think that years acquire
New added joys ?   Dost think thy sire
   More happy than his son ?
That manhood's mirth ?—Oh, go thy ways
To Drury-lane when —— *plays,*
   And see how *forced* our fun !

Thy taws are brave !—thy tops are rare !—
Our tops are spun with coils of care,
   Our *dumps* are no delight !—
The Elgin marbles are but tame,
‘ And ’tis at best a sorry game
   To fly the Muse’s kite !

Our hearts are dough, our heels are lead,
Our topmost joys fall dull and dead
   Like balls with no rebound !
And often with a faded eye
We look behind, and send a sigh
   Towards that merry ground !

Then be contented.   Thou hast got
The most of heaven in thy young lot ;
   There ’s sky-bue in thy cup !
Thou ’lt find thy Manhood all too fast—
Soon come, soon gone ! and Age at last
   A sorry *breaking-up* !

ˈ

MISS KILMANSEGG AND HER PRECIOUS LEG.

A GOLDEN LEGEND.

—◆—

> " What is here?
> Gold ? yellow, glittering, precious gold ? "
>   TIMON OF ATHENS.

Her Pedigree.

To trace the Kilmansegg pedigree,

To the very roots of the family tree,

  Were a task as rash as ridiculous :

Through antediluvian mists as thick

As London fog such a line to pick

Were enough, in truth, to puzzle Old Nick,

  Not to name Sir Harris Nicholas.

It wouldn't require much verbal strain

To trace the Kill-man, perchance, to Cain ;

But waving all such digressions,
Suffice it, according to family lore,
A Patriarch Kilmansegg lived of yore,
Who was famed for his great possessions.

Tradition said he feather'd his nest
Through an Agricultural Interest
In the Golden Age of Farming ;
When golden eggs were laid by the geese,
And Colchian sheep wore a golden fleece,
And golden pippins—the sterling kind
Of Hesperus—now so hard to find—
Made Horticulture quite charming !

A Lord of Land, on his own estate,
He lived at a very lively rate,
But his income would bear carousing ;
Such acres he had of pasture and heath,
With herbage so rich from the ore beneath,
The very ewe's and lambkin's teeth
Were turn'd into gold by browsing.

He gave, without any extra thrift,
A flock of sheep for a birthday gift
   To each son of his loins, or daughter :
And his debts—if debts he had—at will
He liquidated by giving each bill
   A dip in Pactolian water.

'Twas said that even his pigs of lead,
By crossing with some by Midas bred,
   Made a perfect mine of his piggery.
And as for cattle, one yearling bull
Was worth all Smithfield-market full
   Of the Golden Bulls of Pope Gregory.

The high-bred horses within his stud,
Like human creatures of birth and blood,
   Had their Golden Cups and flagons :
And as for the common husbandry nags,
Their noses were tied in money-bags,
   When they stopp'd with the carts and waggons.

Moreover, he had a Golden Ass,
Sometimes at stall, and sometimes at grass,
 That was worth his own weight in money—
And a golden hive, on a Golden Bank,
Where golden bees, by alchemical prank,
 Gather'd gold instead of honey.

Gold! and gold! and gold without end!
He had gold to lay by, and gold to spend,
Gold to give, and gold to lend,
 And reversions of gold *in futuro*.
In wealth the family revell'd and roll'd,
Himself and wife and sons so bold;—
And his daughters sang to their harps of gold
 " O bella eta del' oro! "

Such was the tale of the Kilmansegg Kin,
In golden text on a vellum skin,
Though certain people would wink and grin.

And declare the whole story a parable—
That the Ancestor rich was one Jacob Ghrimes,
Who held a long lease, in prosperous times,
　　Of acres, pasture and arable.

That as money makes money, his golden bees
Were the Five per Cents., or which you please,
　　When his cash was more than plenty—
That the golden cups were racing affairs ;
And his daughters, who sang Italian airs,
　　Had their golden harps of Clementi.

That the Golden Ass, or Golden Bull,
Was English John, with his pockets full,
　　Then at war by land and water :
While beef, and mutton, and other meat,
Were almost as dear as money to eat,
And Farmers reaped Golden Harvests of wheat
　　At the Lord knows what per quarter !

Her Birth.

What different dooms our birthdays bring !
For instance, one little manikin thing
 Survives to wear many a wrinkle ;
While Death forbids another to wake,
And a son that it took nine moons to make
 Expires without even a twinkle !

Into this world we come like ships,
Launch'd from the docks, and stocks, and slips,
 For fortune fair or fatal ;
And one little craft is cast away
In its very first trip in Babbicome Bay,
 While another rides safe at Port Natal.

What different lots our stars accord !
This babe to be hail'd and woo'd as a Lord !
 And that to be shunn'd like a leper !
One, to the world's wine, honey, and corn,
Another, like Colchester native, born
 To its vinegar, only, and pepper.

One is litter'd under a roof
Neither wind nor water proof,—
  That 's the prose of Love in a Cottage,—
A puny, naked, shivering wretch,
The whole of whose birthright would not fetch.
Though Robins himself drew up the sketch,
  The bid of " a mess of pottage."

Born of Fortunatus's kin,
Another comes tenderly usher'd in
  To a prospect all bright and burnish'd :
No tenant he for life's back slums—
He comes to the world as a gentleman comes
  To a lodging ready furnish'd.

And the other sex—the tender—the fair—
What wide reverses of fate are there !
Whilst Margaret, charm'd by the Bulbul rare,
  In a garden of Gul reposes—
Poor Peggy hawks nosegays from street to street,
Till—think of that, who find life so sweet !—
  She hates the smell of roses !

Not so with the infant Kilmansegg !

She was not born to steal or beg,

   Or gather cresses in ditches ;

To plait the straw, or bind the shoe,

Or sit all day to hem and sew,

As females must, and not a few—

   To fill their insides with stitches !

She was not doom'd, for bread to eat,

To be put to her hands as well as her feet—

   To carry home linen from mangles—

Or heavy-hearted, and weary-limb'd,

To dance on a rope in a jacket trimm'd

   With as many blows as spangles.

She was one of those who by Fortune's boon

Are born, as they say, with a silver spoon

   In her mouth, not a wooden ladle :

To speak according to poet's wont,

Plutus as sponsor stood at her font,

   And Midas rock'd the cradle.

At her first *début* she found her head
On a pillow of down, in a downy bed,
  With a damask canopy over.
For although by the vulgar popular saw
All mothers are said to be " in the straw,"
  Some children are born in clover.

Her very first draught of vital air
It was not the common chamelion fare
  Of plebeian lungs and noses,—
    No—her earliest sniff
    Of this world was a whiff
  Of the genuine Otto of Roses !

When she saw the light—it was no mere ray
Of that light so common—so everyday—
  That the sun each morning launches—
But six wax tapers dazzled her eyes,
From a thing—a gooseberry bush for size—
  With a golden stem and branches.

She was born exactly at half-past two,
As witness'd a timepiece in or-molu
    That stood on a marble table—
Showing at once the time of day,
And a team of *Gildings* running away
    As fast as they were able,
With a golden God, with a golden Star,
And a golden Spear, in a golden Car,
    According to Grecian fable.

Like other babes, at her birth she cried :
Which made a sensation far and wide,
    Ay, for twenty miles around her ;
For though to the ear 'twas nothing more
Than an infant's squall, it was really the roar
    Of a Fifty-thousand Pounder !
        It shook the next heir
        In his library chair,
    And made him cry, " Confound her ! "

Of signs and omens there was no dearth,
Any more than at Owen Glendower's birth,

Or the advent of other great people :

Two bullocks dropp'd dead,

As if knock'd on the head,

And barrels of stout

And ale ran about,

And the village-bells such a peal rang out,

That they crack'd the village-steeple.

In no time at all, like mushroom spawn,

Tables sprang up all over the lawn ;

Not furnish'd scantly or shabbily,

But on scale as vast

As that huge repast,

With its loads and cargoes

Of drink and botargoes,

At the Birth of the Babe in Rabelais.

Hundreds of men were turn'd into beasts,

Like the guests at Circe's horrible feasts,

By the magic of ale and cider :

And each country lass, and each country lad,

Began to caper and dance like mad,
And even some old ones appear'd to have had
   A bite from the Naples Spider.

   Then as night came on,
   It had scared King John,
Who considered such signs not risible,
   To have seen the maroons,
   And the whirling moons,
   And the serpents of flame,
   And wheels of the same,
That according to some were " whizzable."

Oh, happy Hope of the Kilmanseggs!
Thrice happy in head, and body, and legs
   That her parents had such full pockets!
For had she been born of Want and Thrift,
For care and nursing all adrift,
It 's ten to one she had had to make shift
   With rickets instead of rockets!

And how was the precious Baby drest ?

In a robe of the East, with lace of the West,

   Like one of Crœsus's issue—

     Her best bibs were made

     Of rich gold brocade,

   And the others of silver tissue.

And when the Baby inclined to nap

She was lull'd on a Gros de Naples lap,

By a nurse in a modish Paris cap,

   Of notions so exalted,

She drank nothing lower than Curaçoa,

Maraschino, or pink Noyau,

   And on principle never malted.

From a golden boat, with a golden spoon,

The babe was fed night, morning, and noon ;

   And altho' the tale seems fabulous,

'Tis said her tops and bottoms were gilt,

Like the oats in that Stable-yard Palace built

   For the horse of Heliogabalus.

And when she took to squall and kick—

For pain will wring and pins will prick

   E'en the wealthiest nabob's daughter—

They gave her no vulgar Dalby or gin,

But a liquor with leaf of gold therein,

   Videlicet,—Dantzic Water.

In short, she was born, and bred, and nurst,

And drest in the best from the very first,

   To please the genteelest censor—

And then, as soon as strength would allow,

Was vaccinated, as babes are now,

With virus ta'en from the best-bred cow

   Of Lord Althorp's—now Earl Spencer.

Her Christening.

Though Shakspeare asks us, " What 's in a name ? "

(As if cognomens were much the same),

   There 's really a very great scope in it.

A name ?—why, wasn 't there Doctor Dodd,

That servant at once of Mammon and God,

Who found four thousand pounds and odd,

    A prison—a cart—and a rope in it ?

A name ?—if the party had a voice,

What mortal would be a Bugg by choice ?

As a Hogg, a Grubb, or a Chubb rejoice ?

    Or any such nauseous blazon ?

Not to mention many a vulgar name,

That would make a doorplate blush for shame,

    If doorplates were not so brazen !

A name ?—it has more than nominal worth,

And belongs to good or bad luck at birth—

    As dames of a certain degree know,

In spite of his Page's hat and hose,

His Page's jacket, and buttons in rows,

Bob only sounds like a page of prose

    Till turn'd into Rupertino.

Now to christen the infant Kilmansegg,

For days and days it was quite a plague,

To hunt the list in the Lexicon :
And scores were tried, like coin, by the ring,
Ere names were found just the proper thing
　For a minor rich as a Mexican.

Then cards were sent, the presence to beg
Of all the kin of Kilmansegg,
　White, yellow, and brown relations :
Brothers, Wardens of City Halls,
And Uncles—rich as three Golden Balls
　From taking pledges of nations.

Nephews, whom Fortune seem'd to bewitch,
　Rising in life like rockets—
Nieces whose doweries knew no hitch—
Aunts as certain of dying rich
　As candles in golden sockets—
Cousins German, and cousin's sons,
All thriving and opulent—some had tons
　Of Kentish hops in their pockets !

For money had stuck to the race through life
(As it did to the bushel when cash so rife
Posed Ali Baba's brother's wife)—
    And down to the Cousins and Coz-lings,
    The fortunate brood of the Kilmanseggs,
    As if they had come out of golden eggs,
        Were all as wealthy as " Goslings."

It would fill a Court Gazette to name
What East and West End people came
    To the rite of Christianity :
    The lofty Lord, and the titled Dame,
        All di'monds, plumes, and urbanity :
His Lordship the May'r with his golden chain,
And two Gold Sticks, and the Sheriffs twain,
Nine foreign Counts, and other great men
With their orders and stars, to help M or N
    To renounce all pomp and vanity.

To paint the maternal Kilmansegg
The pen of an Eastern Poet would beg,

And need an elaborate sonnet ;
How she sparkled with gems whenever she stirr'd,
And her head niddle-noddled at every word,
And seem'd so happy, a Paradise Bird
   Had nidificated upon it.

And Sir Jacob the Father strutted and bow'd,
And smiled to himself, and laugh'd aloud,
   To think of his heiress and daughter—
And then in his pockets he made a grope,
And then, in the fulness of joy and hope,
Seem'd washing his hands with invisible soap,
   In imperceptible water.

He had roll'd in money like pigs in mud,
Till it seem'd to have enter'd into his blood
   By some occult projection :
And his cheeks, instead of a healthy hue,
As yellow as any guinea grew,
Making the common phrase seem true
   About a rich complexion.

And now came the nurse, and during a pause,

Her dead-leaf satin would fitly cause

　　A very autumnal rustle—

So full of figure, so full of fuss,

As she carried about the babe to buss,

　　She seem'd to be nothing but bustle.

A wealthy Nabob was Godpapa,

And an Indian Begum was Godmamma,

　　Whose jewels a Queen might covet—

And the Priest was a Vicar, and Dean withal

Of that Temple we see with a Golden Ball,

　　And a Golden Cross above it.

The Font was a bowl of American gold,

Won by Raleigh in days of old,

　　In spite of Spanish bravado ;

And the Book of Pray'r was so overrun

With gilt devices, it shone in the sun

Like a copy—a presentation one—

　　Of Humboldt's " El Dorado."

Gold ! and gold ! and nothing but gold !

The same auriferous shine behold

   Wherever the eye could settle !

On the walls—the sideboard—the ceiling-sky—

On the gorgeous footmen standing by,

In coats to delight a miner's eye

   With seams of the precious metal.

Gold ! and gold ! and besides the gold,

The very robe of the infant told

A tale of wealth in every fold,

   It lapp'd her like a vapour !

So fine ! so thin ! the mind at a loss

Could compare it to nothing except a cross

   Of cobweb with bank-note paper.

Then her pearls—'twas a perfect sight, forsooth,

To see them, like " the dew of her youth,"

   In such a plentiful sprinkle.

Meanwhile, the Vicar read through the form,

And gave her another, not overwarm,

   That made her little eyes twinkle.

Then the babe was cross'd and bless'd amain ;
But instead of the Kate, or Ann, or Jane,
   Which the humbler female endorses—
Instead of one name, as some people prefix,
Kilmansegg went at the tails of six,
   Like a carriage of state with its horses.

Oh, then the kisses she got and hugs !
The golden mugs and the golden jugs
   That lent fresh rays to the midges !
The golden knives, and the golden spoons,
The gems that sparkled like fairy boons,
It was one of the Kilmansegg's own saloons,
   But look'd like Rundell and Bridge's !

Gold ! and gold ! the new and the old !
The company ate and drank from gold,
   They revell'd, they sang, and were merry ;
And one of the Gold Sticks rose from his chair,
And toasted " the Lass with the golden hair "
   In a bumper of golden Sherry.

Gold! still gold! it rain'd on the nurse,

Who, unlike Danäe, was none the worse ;

There was nothing but guineas glistening!

   Fifty were given to Doctor James,

   For calling the little Baby names,

      And for saying, Amen !

      The Clerk had ten,

And that was the end of the Christening.

Her Childhood.

Our youth ! our childhood ! that spring of springs !

'Tis surely one of the blessedest things

   That nature ever invented !

When the rich are wealthy beyond their wealth,

And the poor are rich in spirits and health,

   And all with their lots contented !

There 's little Phelim, he sings like a thrush,

In the selfsame pair of patchwork plush,

   With the selfsame empty pockets,

That tempted his daddy so often to cut
His throat, or jump in the water-butt—
But what cares Phelim ? an empty nut
 Would sooner bring tears to their sockets.

Give him a collar without a skirt,
That 's the Irish linen for shirt,
And a slice of bread, with a taste of dirt,
 That 's Poverty's Irish butter,
And what does he lack to make him blest ?
Some oyster-shells, or a sparrow's nest.
 A candle-end and a gutter.

But to leave the happy Phelim alone,
Gnawing, perchance, a marrowless bone,
 For which no dog would quarrel—
Turn we to little Miss Kilmansegg,
Cutting her first little toothy-peg
 With a fifty guinea coral—
  A peg upon which
  About poor and rich
 Reflection might hang a moral.

Born in wealth, and wealthily nursed,

Capp'd, papp'd, napp'd and lapp'd from the first

   On the knees of Prodigality,

Her childhood was one eternal round

Of the game of going on Tickler's ground

   Picking up gold—in reality.

With extempore carts she never play'd,

Or the odds and ends of a Tinker's trade,

Or little dirt pies and puddings made,

   Like children happy and squalid ;

The very puppet she had to pet,

Like a bait for the " Nix my Dolly " set,

   Was a Dolly of gold—and solid !

Gold ! and gold ! 'twas the burden still !

To gain the Heiress's early goodwill

   There was much corruption and bribery—

The yearly cost of her golden toys

Would have given half London's Charity Boys

And Charity Girls the annual joys

   Of a holiday dinner at Highbury.

Bon-bons she ate from the gilt cornet ;

And gilded queens on St. Bartlemy's day ;

Till her fancy was tinged by her presents—

And first a goldfinch excited her wish,

Then a spherical bowl with its Golden fish,

And then two Golden Pheasants.

Nay, once she squall'd and scream'd like wild—

And it shows how the bias we give to a child

Is a thing most weighty and solemn :—

But whence was wonder or blame to spring

If little Miss K.,—after such a swing—

Made a dust for the flaming gilded thing

On the top of the Fish Street column ?

Her Education.

According to metaphysical creed,

To the earliest books that children read

For much good or much bad they are debtors—

But before with their A B C they start,

There are things in morals, as well as art,
That play a very important part—
   " Impressions before the letters."

Dame Education begins the pile,
Mayhap in the graceful Corinthian style,
   But alas for the elevation !
If the Lady's maid or Gossip the Nurse
With a load of rubbish, or something worse,
   Have made a rotten foundation.

Even thus with little Miss Kilmansegg,
Before she learnt her E for egg,
   Ere her Governess came, or her Masters—
Teachers of quite a different kind
Had " cramm'd" her beforehand, and put her mind
   In a go-cart on golden castors.

Long before her A B and C,
They had taught her by heart her L. S. D.
   And as how she was born a great Heiress ;
And as sure as London is built of bricks,

My Lord would ask her the day to fix,
To ride in a fine gilt coach and six,
  Like Her Worship the Lady May'ress.

Instead of stories from Edgeworth's page,
The true golden lore for our golden age,
  Or lessons from Barbauld and Trimmer,
Teaching the worth of Virtue and Health,
All that she knew was the Virtue of Wealth,
Provided by vulgar nursery stealth
  With a Book of Leaf Gold for a Primer.

The very metal of merit they told,
And praised her for being as " good as gold ! "
  Till she grew as a peacock haughty ;
Of money they talk'd the whole day round,
And weigh'd desert like grapes by the pound,
Till she had an idea from the very sound
  That people with nought were naughty.

They praised—poor children with nothing at all !
Lord ! how you twaddle and waddle and squall

Like common-bred geese and ganders !
What sad little bad little figures you make
To the rich Miss K., whose plainest seed-cake
    Was stuff'd with corianders !

They praised her falls. as well as her walk.
Flatterers make cream cheese of chalk.
They praised—how they praised—her very small talk.
    As if it fell from a Solon ;
Or the girl who at each pretty phrase let drop
A ruby comma, or pearl full-stop,
    Or an emerald semi-colon.

They praised her spirit, and now and then,
The Nurse brought her own little " nevy " Ben.
    To play with the future May'ress.
And when he got raps, and taps, and slaps.
Scratches, and pinches, snips, and snaps.
    As if from a Tigress or Bearess,
They told him how Lords would court that hand.
And always gave him to understand,

While he rubb'd, poor soul,

His carroty poll,

That his hair had been pull'd by " a *Hairess.*"

Such were the lessons from maid and nurse,

A Governess help'd to make still worse,

Giving an appetite so perverse

    Fresh diet whereon to batten—

Beginning with A. B. C. to hold

Like a royal playbill printed in gold

    On a square of pearl-white satin.

The books to teach the verbs and nouns,

And those about countries, cities, and towns,

Instead of their sober drabs and browns.

    Were in crimson silk, with gilt edges :—

Her Butler, and Eufield, and Entick—in short

Her " Early Lessons " of every sort,

    Look'd like Souvenirs, Keepsakes, and Pledges.

Old Johnson shone out in as fine array

As he did one night when he went to the play :

Chambaud like a beau of King Charles's day—

   Lindley Murray in like conditions—

Each weary, unwelcome, irksome task,

Appear'd in a fancy dress and a mask—

If you wish for similar copies ask

   For Howell and James's Editions.

Novels she read to amuse her mind,

But always the affluent match-making kind

   That ends with Promessi Sposi,

And a father-in-law so wealthy and grand.

He could give cheque-mate to Coutts in the Strand :

   So, along with a ring and posy,

He endows the Bride with Golconda off hand,

   And gives the Groom Potosi.

Plays she perused—but she liked the best

Those comedy gentlefolks always possess'd

   Of fortunes so truly romantic—

Of money so ready that right or wrong

It always is ready to go for a song,

Throwing it, going it, pitching it strong—

They ought to have purses as green and long

As the cucumber called the Gigantic.

Then Eastern Tales she loved for the sake

Of the Purse of Oriental make,

And the thousand pieces they put in it—

But Pastoral scenes on her heart fell cold,

For Nature with her had lost its hold,

No field but the Field of the Cloth of Gold

Would ever have caught her foot in it.

What more?   She learnt to sing, and dance,

To sit on a horse, although he should prance,

And to speak a French not spoken in France

Any more than at Babel's building—

And she painted shells, and flowers, and Turks,

But her great delight was in Fancy Works

That are done with gold or gilding.

Gold ! still gold !—the bright and the dead,

With golden beads, and gold lace, and gold thread

She work'd in gold, as if for her bread ;
  The metal had so undermined her,
Gold ran in her thoughts and fill'd her brain,
She was golden-headed as Peter's cane
  With which he walk'd behind her.

Her Accident.

The horse that carried Miss Kilmansegg,
And a better never lifted leg,
  Was a very rich bay, called Banker—
A horse of a breed and a metal so rare,—
By Bullion out of an Ingot mare,—
That for action, the best of figures, and air,
  It made many good judges hanker.

And when she took a ride in the Park,
Equestrian Lord, or pedestrian Clerk,
  Was thrown in an amorous fever,
To see the Heiress how well she sat,
With her groom behind her, Bob or Nat,
In green, half smother'd with gold, and a hat
  With more gold lace than beaver.

And then when Banker obtain'd a pat,

To see how he arch'd his neck at that !

　　He snorted with pride and pleasure !

Like the Steed in the fable so lofty and grand,

Who gave the poor Ass to understand,

That *he* didn't carry a bag of sand,

　　But a burden of golden treasure.

A load of treasure ?—alas ! alas !

Had her horse but been fed upon English grass,

　　And sheltered in Yorkshire spinneys,

Had he scour'd the sand with the Desart Ass,

　　Or where the American whinnies—

But a hunter from Erin's turf and gorse,

A regular thorough-bred Irish horse,

Why, he ran away, as a matter of course,

　　With a girl worth her weight in guineas !

Mayhap 'tis the trick of such pamper'd nags

To shy at the sight of a beggar in rags,

　　But away, like the bolt of a rabbit,

Away went the horse in the madness of fright.

And away went the horsewoman mocking the sight—
Was yonder blue flash a flash of blue light,
  Or only the skirt of her habit ?

Away she flies, with the groom behind,—
It looks like a race of the Calmuck kind,
  When Hymen himself is the starter :
And the Maid rides first in the fourfooted strife,
Riding, striding, as if for her life,
While the Lover rides after to catch him a wife,
  Although it 's catching a Tartar.

But the Groom has lost his glittering hat !
Though he does not sigh and pull up for that—
Alas ! his horse is a tit for Tat
  To sell to a very low bidder—
His wind is ruin'd, his shoulder is sprung,
Things, though a horse be handsome and young,
  A purchaser *will* consider.

But still flies the Heiress through stones and dust.
Oh, for a fall, if fall she must,

On the gentle lap of Flora !

But still, thank Heaven ! she clings to her seat—

Away ! away ! she could ride a dead heat

With the Dead who ride so fast and fleet,

    In the Ballad of Leonora !

Away she gallops !—it's awful work !

It 's faster than Turpin's ride to York,

    On Bess that notable clipper !

She has circled the Ring !—she crosses the Park !

Mazeppa, although he was stripp'd so stark,

    Mazeppa couldn 't outstrip her !

The fields seem running away with the folks !

The Elms are having a race for the Oaks !

    At a pace that all Jockeys disparages !

All, all is racing ! the Serpentine

Seems rushing past like the " arrowy Rhine,"

The houses have got on a railway line,

    And are off like the first-class carriages !

She 'll lose her life ! she is losing her breath !

A cruel chase, she is chasing Death,

   As female shriekings forewarn her :

And now—as gratis as blood of Guelph—

She clears that gate, which has clear'd itself

   Since then, at Hyde Park Corner !

Alas ! for the hope of the Kilmanseggs !

For her head, her brains, her body, and legs,

   Her life 's not worth a copper !

     Willy-nilly,

     In Piccadilly,

A hundred hearts turn sick and chilly,

   A hundred voices cry, " Stop her ! "

And one old gentleman stares and stands,

Shakes his head and lifts his hands,

   And says, " How very improper ! "

On and on !—what a perilous run !

The iron rails seem all mingling in one.

   To shut out the Green Park scenery !

And now the Cellar its dangers reveals,

She shudders—she shrieks—she 's doom'd, she feels,
To be torn by powers of horses and wheels,
    Like a spinner by steam machinery !

Sick with horror she shuts her eyes,
But the very stones seem uttering cries,
    As they did to that Persian daughter,
When she climb'd up the steep vociferous hill,
Her little silver flagon to fill
    With the magical Golden Water !

" Batter her ! shatter her !
Throw and scatter her ! "
Shouts each stony-hearted chatterer—
    " Dash at the heavy Dover !
Spill her ! kill her ! tear and tatter her !
Smash her ! crash her ! " (the stones didn 't flatter
        her !)
" Kick her brains out ! let her blood spatter her !
    Roll on her over and over ! "

For so she gather'd the awful sense
Of the street in its past unmacadamized tense,
   As the wild horse overran it,—
His four heels making the clatter of six,
Like a Devil's tattoo, played with iron sticks
   On a kettle-drum of granite!

On! still on! she 's dazzled with hints
Of oranges, ribbons, and colour'd prints,
A Kaleidoscope jumble of shapes and tints.
   And human faces all flashing,
Bright and brief as the sparks from the flints.
   That the desperate hoof keeps dashing!

On and on! still frightfully fast!
Dover-street, Bond-street, all are past!
But—yes—no—yes!—they 're down at last!
   The Furies and Fates have found them!
Down they go with a sparkle and crash,
Like a Bark that 's struck by the lightning flash—

There 's a shriek—and a sob—

And the dense dark mob

Like a billow closes around them !

*   *   *   *   *

    *   *   *   *

" She breathes ! "

" She don't ! "

" She 'll recover ! "

" She won't ! "

" She 's stirring ! she 's living, by Nemesis ! "

Gold, still gold ! on counter and shelf !

Golden dishes as plenty as delf !

Miss Kilmansegg 's coming again to herself

    On an opulent Goldsmith's premises !

Gold ! fine gold !—both yellow and red,

Beaten, and molten—polish'd, and dead—

To see the gold with profusion spread

    In all forms of its manufacture !

But what avails gold to Miss Kilmansegg,

When the femoral bone of her dexter leg

    Has met with a compound fracture ?

Gold may sooth Adversity's smart :

Nay, help to bind up a broken heart ;

But to try it on any other part

    Were as certain a disappointment,

As if one should rub the dish and plate.

Taken out of a Staffordshire crate—

In the hope of a Golden Service of State—

    With Singleton's " Golden Ointment."

Her Precious Leg.

" As the twig is bent, the tree 's inclined,"

Is an adage often recall'd to mind,

    Referring to juvenile bias :

And never so well is the verity seen,

As when to the weak, warp'd side we lean,

    While Life 's tempests and hurricanes try us.

Even thus with Miss K. and her broken limb,

By a very, very remarkable whim,

    She show'd her early tuition :

While the buds of character came into blow

With a certain tinge that served to show
The nursery culture long ago,
  As the graft is known by fruition !

For the King's Physician, who nursed the case,
His verdict gave with an awful face,
  And three others concurr'd to egg it ;
That the Patient to give old Death the slip,
Like the Pope, instead of a personal trip,
  Must send her Leg as a Legate.

The limb was doom'd—it couldn't be saved !
And like other people the patient behaved,
Nay, bravely that cruel parting braved,
  Which makes some persons so falter,
They rather would part, without a groan,
With the flesh of their flesh, and bone of their bone,
  They obtain'd at St. George's altar.

But when it came to fitting the stump
With a proxy limb—then flatly and plump
  She spoke, in the spirit olden ;

She couldn't—she shouldn't—she wouldn't have
  wood !
Nor a leg of cork, if she never stood,
And she swore an oath, or something as good,
  The proxy limb should be golden !

A wooden leg ! what, a sort of peg,
  For your common Jockeys and Jennies !
No, no, her mother might worry and plague—
Weep, go down on her knees, and beg,
But nothing would move Miss Kilmansegg !
She could—she would have a Golden Leg,
  If it cost ten thousand guineas !

Wood indeed, in Forest or Park,
With its sylvan honours and feudal bark,
  Is an aristocratical article :
But split and sawn, and hack'd about town,
Serving all needs of pauper or clown,
Trod on ! stagger'd on ! Wood cut down
  Is vulgar—fibre and particle !

And Cork !—when the noble Cork Tree shades
A lovely group of Castilian maids,
     'Tis a thing for a song or sonnet!—
But cork, as it stops the bottle of gin,
Or bungs the beer—the *small* beer—in,
It pierced her heart like a corking-pin,
     To think of standing upon it !

A Leg of Gold—solid gold throughout,
Nothing else, whether slim or stout,
     Should ever support her, God willing !
She must—she could—she would have her whim,
Her father, she turn'd a deaf ear to him—
     He might kill her—she didn't mind killing !
He was welcome to cut off her other limb—
     He might cut her all off with a shilling !

All other promised gifts were in vain,
Golden Girdle, or Golden Chain,
She writhed with impatience more than pain,
     And utter'd " pshaws ! " and " pishes ! "

But a Leg of Gold ! as she lay in bed,

It danced before her—it ran in her head !

  It jump'd with her dearest wishes !

"Gold—gold—gold !   Oh, let it be gold ! "

Asleep or awake that tale she told,

  And when she grew delirious :

Till her parents resolved to grant her wish,

If they melted down plate, and goblet, and dish,

  The case was getting so serious.

So a Leg was made in a comely mould,

Of Gold, fine virgin glittering gold,

  As solid as man could make it—

Solid in foot, and calf, and shank,

A prodigious sum of money it sank ;

In fact 'twas a Branch of the family Bank,

  And no easy matter to break it.

All sterling metal—not half-and half,

The Goldsmith's mark was stamp'd on the calf—

  'Twas pure as from Mexican barter !

And to make it more costly, just over the knee,

Where another ligature used to be,

Was a circle of jewels, worth shillings to see,

    A new-fangled Badge of the Garter!

'Twas a splendid, brilliant, beautiful Leg,

Fit for the Court of Scander-Beg,

That Precious Leg of Miss Kilmansegg!

    For, thanks to parental bounty,

Secure from Mortification's touch,

She stood on a Member that cost as much

    As a Member for all the County!

Her Fame.

To gratify stern ambition's whims,

What hundreds and thousands of precious limbs

    On a field of battle we scatter!

Sever'd by sword, or bullet, or saw,

Off they go, all bleeding and raw,—

But the public seems to get the lock-jaw,

    So little is said on the matter!

Legs, the tightest that ever were seen,

The tightest, the lightest, that danced on the green,

   Cutting capers to sweet Kitty Clover ;

Shatter'd, scatter'd, cut, and bowl'd down,

Off they go, worse off for renown,

A line in the *Times*, or a talk about town,

   Than the leg that a fly runs over !

But the Precious Leg of Miss Kilmansegg,

That gowden, goolden, golden leg,

   Was the theme of all conversation !

Had it been a Pillar of Church and State,

Or a prop to support the whole Dead Weight,

It could not have furnish'd more debate

   To the heads and tails of the nation !

East and west, and north and south,

Though useless for either hunger or drouth,—

The Leg was in every body's mouth,

   To use a poetical figure,

Rumour, in taking her ravenous swim,

Saw, and seized on the tempting limb,

   Like a shark on the leg of a nigger.

Wilful murder fell very dead ;

Debates in the House were hardly read ;

In vain the Police Reports were fed

   With Irish riots and *rumpuses*—

The Leg ! the Leg ! was the great event,

Through every circle in life it went,

   Like the leg of a pair of compasses.

The last new Novel seem'd tame and flat.

The Leg, a novelty newer than that,

   Had tripp'd up the heels of Fiction !

It Burked the very essays of Burke,

And, alas ! how Wealth over Wit plays the Turk !

As a regular piece of goldsmith's work,

   Got the better of Goldsmith's diction.

" A leg of gold ! what of solid gold ? "

Cried rich and poor, and young and old,—

And Master and Miss and Madam—
'Twas the talk of 'Change—the Alley—the Bank—
And with men of scientific rank,
It made as much stir as the fossil shank
    Of a Lizard coeval with Adam !

Of course with Greenwich and Chelsea elves,
Men who had lost a limb themselves,
    Its interest did not dwindle—
But Bill, and Ben, and Jack, and Tom
Could hardly have spun more yarns therefrom,
    If the leg had been a spindle.

Meanwhile the story went to and fro,
Till, gathering like the ball of snow,
By the time it got to Stratford-le-Bow,
    Through Exaggeration's touches,
The Heiress and Hope of the Kilmanseggs
Was propp'd on *two* fine Golden Legs,
    And a pair of Golden Crutches!

Never had Leg so great a run !

'Twas the " go " and the " Kick " thrown into one !

The mode—the new thing under the sun,

The rage—the fancy—the passion !

Bonnets were named, and hats were worn,

A la Golden Leg instead of Leghorn,

And stockings and shoes,

Of golden hues,

Took the lead in the walks of fashion !

The Golden Leg had a vast career,

It was sung and danced—and to show how near

Low Folly to lofty approaches,

Down to society's very dregs,

The Belles of Wapping wore "Kilmanseggs,"

And St. Giles's Beaux sported Golden Legs

In their pinchbeck pins and brooches !

Her First Step.

Supposing the Trunk and Limbs of Man

Shared, on the allegorical plan,

By the Passions that mark Humanity,
Whichever might claim the head, or heart,
The stomach, or any other part,
  The Legs would be seized by Vanity.

There 's Bardus, a six-foot column of fop,
A lighthouse without any light atop,
  Whose height would attract beholders,
If he had not lost some inches clear
By looking down at his kerseymere,
Ogling the limbs he holds so dear,
  Till he got a stoop in his shoulders.

Talk of Art, of Science, or Books,
And down go the everlasting looks,
  To his crural beauties so wedded !
Try him, wherever you will, you find
His mind in his legs, and his legs in his mind,
All prongs and folly—in short a kind
  Of Fork—that is Fiddle-headed.

What wonder, then, if Miss Kilmansegg,

With a splendid, brilliant, beautiful leg,

Fit for the court of Scander-Beg,

Disdain'd to hide it like Joan or Meg,

 In petticoats stuff'd or quilted ?

Not she ! 'twas her convalescent whim

To dazzle the world with her precious limb,—

 Nay, to go a little high-kilted.

So cards were sent for that sort of mob

Where Tartars and Africans hob-and-nob,

And the Cherokee talks of his cab and cob

 To Polish or Lapland lovers—

Cards like that hieroglyphical call

To a geographical Fancy Ball

 On the recent Post-Office covers.

For if Lion-hunters—and great ones too—

Would mob a savage from Latakoo,

Or squeeze for a glimpse of Prince Le Boo,

 That unfortunate Sandwich scion—

Hundreds of first-rate people, no doubt,

Would gladly, madly, rush to a rout,

  That promised a Golden Lion!

Her Fancy Ball.

Of all the spirits of evil fame

That hurt the soul or injure the frame,

  And poison what 's honest and hearty,

There 's none more needs a Mathew to preach

A cooling, antiphlogistic speech,

      To praise and enforce

      A temperate course,

  Than the Evil Spirit of Party.

Go to the House of Commons, or Lords,

And they seem to be busy with simple words

  In their popular sense or pedantic—

But, alas! with their cheers, and sneers, and jeers,

They 're really busy, whatever appears,

  Putting peas in each other's ears,

    To drive their enemies frantic!

Thus Tories love to worry the Whigs,

Who treat them in turn like Schwalbach pigs,

Giving them lashes, thrashes, and digs,

   With their writhing and pain delighted—

But after all that 's said, and more,

The malice and spite of Party are poor

To the malice and spite of a party next door,

   To a party not invited.

On with the cap and out with the light,

Weariness bids the world good night,

   At least for the usual season ;

But hark ! a clatter of horses' heels ;

And Sleep and Silence are broken on wheels,

   Like Wilful Murder and Treason !

Another crash—and the carriage goes—

Again poor Weariness seeks the repose

   That Nature demands imperious ;

But Echo takes up the burden now,

With a rattling chorus of row-de-dow-dow,

Till Silence herself seems making a row,

   Like a Quaker gone delirious !

'Tis night—a winter night—and the stars

Are shining like winkin'—Venus and Mars

Are rolling along in their golden cars

   Through the sky's serene expansion—

But vainly the stars dispense their rays,

Venus and Mars are lost in the blaze

   Of the Kilmanseggs' luminous mansion !

Up jumps Fear in a terrible fright !

His bedchamber windows look so bright,

   With light all the Square is glutted !

Up he jumps, like a sole from the pan,

And a tremor sickens his inward man,

For he feels as only a gentleman can,

   Who thinks he 's being " gutted."

Again Fear settles, all snug and warm ;

But only to dream of a dreadful storm

From Autumn's sulphurous locker;
But the only electric body that falls,
Wears a negative coat, and positive smalls,
And draws the peal that so appals
    From the Kilmanseggs' brazen knocker!

'Tis Curiosity's Benefit night—
And perchance 'tis the English Second-Sight,
    But whatever it be, so be it—
As the friends and guests of Miss Kilmansegg
Crowd in to look at her Golden Leg,
        As many more
        Mob round the door,
    To see them going to see it!

In they go—in jackets, and cloaks,
Plumes, and bonnets, turbans, and toques,
    As if to a Congress of Nations :
Greeks and Malays, with daggers and dirks,
Spaniards, Jews, Chinese, and Turks—
Some like original foreign works.
    But mostly like bad translations.

In they go, and to work like a pack,
Juan, Moses, and Shacabac,
  Tom, and Jerry, and Springheel'd Jack,
For some of low Fancy are lovers—
Skirting, zigzagging, casting about,
Here and there, and in and out,
With a crush, and a rush, for a full-bodied rout
  In one of the stiffest of covers.

In they went, and hunted about.
Open mouth'd like chub and trout,
And some with the upper lip thrust out,
  Like that fish for routing, a barbel—
While Sir Jacob stood to welcome the crowd,
And rubb'd his hands, and smiled aloud,
And bow'd, and bow'd, and bow'd, and bow'd,
  Like a man who is sawing marble.

For Princes were there, and Noble Peers ;
Dukes descended from Norman spears ;
Earls that dated from early years ;
  And Lords in vast variety—

Besides the Gentry both new and old—
For people who stand on legs of gold,
   Are sure to stand well with society.

" But where—where—where ? " with one accord
Cried Moses and Mufti, Jack and my Lord,
   Wang-Fong and Il Boudocani—
When slow, and heavy, and dead as a dump,
They heard a foot begin to stump,
      Thump ! lump !
      Lump ! thump !
   Like the Spectre in " Don Giovanni ! "

And lo ! the Heiress, Miss Kilmansegg,
With her splendid, brilliant, beautiful leg,
   In the garb of a Goddess olden—
Like chaste Diana going to hunt,
With a golden spear—which of course was blunt,
And a tunic loop'd up to a gem in front,
   To shew the Leg that was Golden !

Gold ! still gold ! her Crescent behold,

That should be silver, but would be gold ;

   And her robe's auriferous spangles!

Her golden stomacher—how she would melt !

Her golden quiver, and golden belt,

   Where a golden bugle dangles !

And her jewell'd Garter ? Oh, Sin ! Oh, Shame !

Let Pride and Vanity bear the blame.

That bring such blots on female fame !

   But to be a true recorder,

Besides its thin transparent stuff,

The tunic was loop'd quite high enough

   To give a glimpse of the Order !

But what have sin or shame to do

With a Golden Leg—and a stout one too?

   Away with all Prudery's panics !

That the precious metal, by thick and thin,

Will cover square acres of land or sin,

Is a fact made plain

Again and again,

In Morals as well as Mechanics.

A few, indeed, of her proper sex,

Who seem'd to feel her foot on their necks,

And fear'd their charms would meet with checks

    From so rare and splendid a blazon—

A few cried " fie ! "—and " forward "—and "bold ! "

And said of the Leg it might be gold,

    But to them it looked like brazen !

'Twas hard they hinted for flesh and blood,

Virtue, and Beauty, and all that's good,

    To strike to mere dross their topgallants—

But what were Beauty, or Virtue, or Worth,

Gentle manners, or gentle birth,

Nay, what the most talented head on earth

    To a Leg worth fifty Talents !

But the men sang quite another hymn

Of glory and praise to the precious Limb—

Age, sordid Age, admired the whim,

   And its indecorum pardon'd—

While half of the young—ay, more than half—

Bow'd down and worshipp'd the Golden Calf,

   Like the Jews when their hearts were harden'd.

A Golden Leg! what fancies it fired!

What golden wishes and hopes inspired!

   To give but a mere abridgement—

What a leg to leg-bail Embarrassment's serf!

What a leg for a Leg to take on the turf!

   What a leg for a marching regiment!

A Golden Leg!—whatever Love sings,

'Twas worth a bushel of " Plain Gold Rings "

   With which the Romantic wheedles.

'Twas worth all the legs in stockings and socks—

'Twas a leg that might be put in the Stocks,

   N.B.—Not the parish beadle's!

And Lady K. nid-nodded her head,

Lapp'd in a turban fancy-bred,

Just like a love-apple, huge and red,
　　Some Mussul-womanish mystery ;
　　　But whatever she meant
　　　　To represent,
　　She talk'd like the Muse of History.

She told how the filial leg was lost :
And then how much the gold one cost ;
　　With its weight to a Trojan fraction :
And how it took off, and how it put on ;
And call'd on Devil, Duke, and Don,
Mahomet, Moses, and Prester John,
　　To notice its beautiful action.

And then of the Leg she went in quest :
And led it where the light was best ;
And made it lay itself up to rest
　　In postures for painters' studies :
It cost more tricks and trouble by half,
Than it takes to exhibit a Six-legg'd Calf
　　To a boothful of country Cuddies.

Nor yet did the Heiress herself omit

The arts that help to make a hit,

   And preserve a prominent station.

She talk'd and laugh'd far more than her share :

And took a part in " Rich and Rare

Were the gems she wore "—and the gems were there,

   Like a Song with an Illustration.

She even stood up with a Count of France

To dance—alas ! the measures we dance

   When Vanity plays the Piper !

Vanity, Vanity, apt to betray,

And lead all sorts of legs astray,

Wood, or metal, or human clay,—

   Since Satan first play'd the Viper !

But first she doff'd her hunting gear,

And favour'd Tom Tug with her golden spear.

   To row with down the river—

A Bonze had her golden bow to hold ;

A Hermit her belt and bugle of gold ;

   And an Abbot her golden quiver.

And then a space was clear'd on the floor,

And she walk'd the Minuet de la Cour,

With all the pomp of a Pompadour,

But although she began *andante*,

Conceive the faces of all the Rout,

When she finish'd off with a whirligig bout,

And the Precious Leg stuck stiffly out

Like the leg of a *Figurante*!

So the courtly dance was goldenly done,

And golden opinions, of course, it won

From all different sorts of people—

Chiming, ding-dong, with flattering phrase,

In one vociferous peal of praise,

Like the peal that rings on Royal days

From Loyalty's parish-steeple.

And yet, had the leg been one of those

That dance for bread in flesh-colour'd hose,

With Rosina's pastoral bevy,

The jeers it had met,—the shouts ! the scoff !
The cutting advice to "take itself off,"
  For sounding but half so heavy.

Had it been a leg like those, perchance,
That teach little girls and boys to dance,
To set, poussette, recede, and advance,
  With the steps and figures most proper,—
Had it hopp'd for a weekly or quarterly sum,
How little of praise or grist would have come
  To a mill with such a hopper !

But the Leg was none of those limbs forlorn—
Bartering capers and hops for corn—
That meet with public hisses and scorn,
  Or the morning journal denounces—
Had it pleas'd to caper from morn till dusk,
There was all the music of " Money Musk "
  In its ponderous bangs and bounces.

But hark !—as slow as the strokes of a pump,

Lump, thump!

Thump, lump !

As the Giant of Castle Otranto might stump

To a lower room from an upper—

Down she goes with a noisy dint,

For taking the crimson turban's hint,

A noble Lord at the Head of the Mint

Is leading the Leg to supper !

But the supper, alas ! must rest untold,

With its blaze of light and its glitter of gold,

For to paint that scene of glamour,

It would need the Great Enchanter's charm,

Who waves over Palace, and Cot, and Farm,

An arm like the Goldbeater's Golden Arm

That wields a Golden Hammer.

He—only HE—could fitly state

THE MASSIVE SERVICE OF GOLDEN PLATE,

With the proper phrase and expansion—

The Rare Selection of FOREIGN WINES—

The ALPS OF ICE and MOUNTAINS OF PINES,

The punch in OCEANS and sugary shrines,

The TEMPLE OF TASTE from GUNTER'S
    DESIGNS—

In short, all that WEALTH with A FEAST com-
    bines,

    In a SPLENDID FAMILY MANSION.

Suffice it each mask'd outlandish guest

Ate and drank of the very best,

    According to critical conners—

And then they pledged the Hostess and Host,

But the Golden Leg was the standing toast,

      And as somebody swore,

      Walk'd off with more

    Than its share of the " Hips ! " and honours !

      "Miss Kilmansegg !—

      Full glasses I beg !—

Miss Kilmansegg and her Precious Leg ! "

    And away went the bottle careering !

Wine in bumpers ! and shouts in peals !

Till the Clown didn't know his head from his heels,

The Mussulman's eyes danced two-some reels,

   And the Quaker was hoarse with cheering !

Her Dream.

Miss Kilmansegg took off her leg,

And laid it down like a cribbage-peg,

   For the Rout was done and the riot :

The Square was hush'd ; not a sound was heard ;

The sky was gray, and no creature stirr'd,

Except one little precocious bird,

   That chirp'd—and then was quiet.

So still without,—so still within ;—

   It had been a sin

   To drop a pin—

So intense is silence after a din,

   It seem'd like Death's rehearsal!

To stir the air no eddy came ;

And the taper burnt with as still a flame,
As to flicker had been a burning shame,
   In a calm so universal.

The time for sleep had come at last ;
And there was the bed, so soft, so vast,
   Quite a field of Bedfordshire clover ;
Softer, cooler, and calmer, no doubt,
From the piece of work just ravell'd out,
For one of the pleasures of having a rout
   Is the pleasure of having it over.

No sordid pallet, or truckle mean,
Of straw, and rug, and tatters unclean ;
But a splendid, gilded, carved machine,
   That was fit for a Royal Chamber.
On the top was a gorgeous golden wreath ;
And the damask curtains hung beneath,
   Like clouds of crimson and amber.

Curtains, held up by two little plump things,
With golden bodies and golden wings,—
    Mere fins for such solidities—
        Two Cupids, in short,
        Of the regular sort,
    But the housemaid call'd them " Cupidities."

No patchwork quilt, all seams and scars,
But velvet, powder'd with golden stars,
    A fit mantle for *Night*-Commanders !
And the pillow, as white as snow undimm'd,
And as cool as the pool that the breeze has skimm'd,
Was eased in the finest cambric, and trimm'd
    With the costliest lace of Flanders.

And the bed—of the Eider's softest down,
'Twas a place to revel, to smother, to drown
    In a bliss inferr'd by the Poet ;
For if Ignorance be indeed a bliss,
What blessed ignorance equals this,
    To sleep—and not to know it ?

Oh, bed ! oh, bed ! delicious bed !

That heaven upon earth to the weary head ;

But a place that to name would be ill-bred,

To the head with a wakeful trouble—

'Tis held by such a different lease !

To one, a place of comfort and peace,

All stuff'd with the down of stubble geese,

To another with only the stubble !

To one, a perfect Halcyon nest,

All calm, and balm, and quiet, and rest,

And soft as the fur of the cony—

To another, so restless for body and head,

That the bed seems borrow'd from Nettlebed,

And the pillow from Stratford the Stony !

To the happy, a first-class carriage of ease,

To the Land of Nod, or where you please ;

But alas ! for the watchers and weepers.

Who turn, and turn, and turn again,

But turn, and turn, and turn in vain,

With an anxious brain,

And thoughts in a train

That does not run upon *sleepers!*

Wide awake as the mousing owl,

Night-hawk, or other nocturnal fowl,—

   But more profitless vigils keeping,—

Wide awake in the dark they stare,

Filling with phantoms the vacant air,

As if that Crook-back'd Tyrant Care

   Had plotted to kill them sleeping.

And oh! when the blessed diurnal light

Is quench'd by the providential night,

   To render our slumber more certain,

Pity, pity the wretches that weep,

For they must be wretched who cannot sleep

   When God himself draws the curtain!

The careful Betty the pillow beats,

And airs the blankets, and smoothes the sheets,

   And gives the mattress a shaking—

But vainly Betty performs her part,
If a ruffled head and a rumpled heart
  As well as the couch want making.

There 's Morbid, all bile, and verjuice, and nerves,
Where other people would make preserves,
  He turns his fruits into pickles :
Jealous, envious, and fretful by day,
At night, to his own sharp fancies a prey,
He lies like a hedgehog rolled up the wrong way,
  Tormenting himself with his prickles.

But a child—that bids the world good night,
In downright earnest and cuts it quite—
  A Cherub no Art can copy,—
'Tis a perfect picture to see him lie
As if he had supp'd on dormouse pie,
(An ancient classical dish by the by)
  With a sauce of syrup of poppy.

Oh, bed ! bed ! bed ! delicious bed !
That heav'n upon earth to the weary head,

Whether lofty or low its condition!
But instead of putting our plagues on shelves,
In our blankets how often we toss ourselves,
Or are toss'd by such allegorical elves
   As Pride, Hate, Greed, and Ambition!

The independent Miss Kilmansegg
Took off her independent Leg
   And laid it beneath her pillow,
And then on the bed her frame she cast,
The time for repose had come at last,
But long, long, after the storm is past
   Rolls the turbid, turbulent billow.

No part she had in vulgar cares
That belong to common household affairs—
Nocturnal annoyances such as theirs
   Who lie with a shrewd surmising
That while they are couchant (a bitter cup!)
Their bread and butter are getting up,
   And the coals—confound them!—are rising.

No fear she had her sleep to postpone,
Like the crippled Widow who weeps alone,
And cannot make a doze her own,
    For the dread that mayhap on the morrow,
The true and Christian reading to balk,
A broker will take up her bed and walk,
    By way of curing her sorrow.

No cause like these she had to bewail :
But the breath of applause had blown a gale,
And winds from that quarter seldom fail
    To cause some human commotion ;
But whenever such breezes coincide
        With the very spring-tide
        Of human pride,
    There 's no such swell on the ocean !

Peace, and ease, and slumber lost,
She turn'd, and roll'd, and tumbled, and toss'd,
    With a tumult that would not settle :

A common case, indeed, with such
As have too little, or think too much,
  Of the precious and glittering metal.

Gold!—she saw at her golden foot
The Peer whose tree had an olden root,
The Proud, the Great, the Learned to boot,
  The handsome, the gay, and the witty—
The Man of Science—of Arms—of Art,
The man who deals but at Pleasure's mart,
  And the man who deals in the City.

Gold, still gold—and true to the mould!
In the very scheme of her dream it told :
  For, by magical transmutation,
From her Leg through her body it seem'd to go,
Till, gold above, and gold below,
She was gold, all gold, from her little gold toe
  To her organ of Veneration!

And still she retain'd, through Fancy's art,

The Golden Bow, and the Golden Dart,

With which she had played a Goddess's part

In her recent glorification.

And still, like one of the self-same brood,

On a Plinth of the self-same metal she stood

For the whole world's adoration.

And hymns of incense around her roll'd,

From Golden Harps and Censers of Gold,—

For Fancy in dreams is as uncontroll'd

As a horse without a bridle :

What wonder, then, from all checks exempt,

If, inspired by the Golden Leg, she dreamt

She was turn'd to a Golden Idol ?

Her Courtship.

When leaving Eden's happy land

The grieving Angel led by the hand

Our banish'd Father and Mother,

Forgotten amid their awful doom,

The tears, the fears, and the future's gloom,
On each brow was a wreath of Paradise bloom,
   That our Parents had twined for each other.

It was only while sitting like figures of stone,
For the grieving Angel had skyward flown,
As they sat, those Two, in the world alone,
   With disconsolate hearts nigh cloven,
That scenting the gust of happier hours,
They look'd around for the precious flow'rs,
And lo !—a last relic of Eden's dear bow'rs—
   The chaplet that Love had woven !

And still, when a pair of Lovers meet,
There 's a sweetness in air, unearthly sweet,
That savours still of that happy retreat
   Where Eve by Adam was courted :
Whilst the joyous Thrush, and the gentle Dove,
Woo'd their mates in the boughs above,
   And the Serpent, as yet, only sported.

Who hath not felt that breath in the air,

A perfume and freshness strange and rare,

A warmth in the light, and a bliss every where,

   When young hearts yearn together?

All sweets below, and all sunny above,

Oh! there's nothing in life like making love,

   Save making hay in fine weather!

Who hath not found amongst his flow'rs

A blossom too bright for this world of ours,

   Like a rose among snows of Sweden?

But to turn again to Miss Kilmansegg,

Where must Love have gone to beg,

If such a thing as a Golden Leg

   Had put its foot in Eden!

And yet—to tell the rigid truth—

Her favour was sought by Age and Youth—

   For the prey will find a prowler!

She was follow'd, flatter'd, courted, address'd,

Woo'd, and coo'd, and wheedled, and press'd.

By suitors from North, South, East, and West.

   Like that Heiress, in song, Tibbie Fowler!

But, alas! alas! for the Woman's fate,

Who has from a mob to choose a mate!

   'Tis a strange and painful mystery!

But the more the eggs, the worse the hatch;

The more the fish, the worse the catch;

The more the sparks, the worse the match;

   Is a fact in Woman's history.

Give her between a brace to pick.

And, mayhap, with luck to help the trick,

She will take the Faustus, and leave the Old Nick—

   But her future bliss to baffle,

Amongst a score let her have a voice,

And she 'll have as little cause to rejoice,

As if she had won the " Man of her choice "

   In a matrimonial raffle!

Thus, even thus, with the Heiress and Hope,
Fulfilling the adage of too much rope,
  With so ample a competition,
She chose the least worthy of all the group,
Just as the vulture makes a stoop,
And singles out from the herd or troop
  The beast of the worst condition.

A Foreign Count—who came incog..
Not under a cloud, but under a fog,
  In a Calais packet's fore-cabin,
To charm some lady British-born,
With his eyes as black as the fruit of the thorn,
And his hooky nose, and his beard half-shorn,
  Like a half-converted Rabbin.

And because the Sex confess a charm
In the man who has slash'd a head or arm,
  Or has been a throat's undoing,
He was dress'd like one of the glorious trade,

At least when glory is off parade,
With a stock, and a frock, well trimm'd with braid,
And frogs—that went a-wooing.

Moreover, as Counts are apt to do,
On the left-hand side of his dark surtout,
At one of those holes that buttons go through.
    (To be a precise recorder,)
A ribbon he wore, or rather a scrap,
About an inch of ribbon mayhap,
That one of his rivals, a whimsical chap,
    Described as his " Retail Order."

And then—and much it help'd his chance—
He could sing, and play first fiddle, and dance,
Perform charades, and Proverbs of France—
    Act the tender, and do the cruel ;
For amongst his other killing parts,
He had broken a brace of female hearts,
    And murder'd three men in duel !

Savage at heart, and false of tongue,

Subtle with age, and smooth to the young,

　　Like a snake in his coiling and curling—

Such was the Count—to give him a niche—

Who came to court that Heiress rich,

And knelt at her foot—one needn't say which—

　　Besieging her Castle of *Sterling*.

With pray'rs and vows he open'd his trench,

And plied her with English, Spanish, and French,

　　In phrases the most sentimental :

And quoted poems in High and Low Dutch,

With now and then an Italian touch,

Till she yielded, without resisting much,

　　To homage so continental.

And then the sordid bargain to close,

With a miniature sketch of his hooky nose,

And his dear dark eyes, as black as sloes,

And his beard and whiskers as black as those.

The lady's consent he requited—
And instead of the lock that lovers beg,
The Count received from Miss Kilmansegg
A model, in small, of her Precious Leg—
    And so the couple were plighted!

But, oh! the love that gold must crown!
Better—better, the love of the clown,
Who admires his lass in her Sunday gown,
    As if all the fairies had dress'd her!
Whose brain to no crooked thought gives birth,
Except that he never will part on earth
    With his true love's crooked tester!

Alas! for the love that 's link'd with gold!
Better—better a thousand times told—
    More honest, happy, and laudable,
The downright loving of pretty Cis,
Who wipes her lips, though there 's nothing amiss,
And takes a kiss, and gives a kiss,
    In which her heart is audible!

Pretty Cis, so smiling and bright,

Who loves as she labours, with all her might,

   And without any sordid leaven !

Who blushes as red as haws and hips,

Down to her very finger-tips,

For Roger's blue ribbons—to her, like strips

   Cut out of the azure of Heaven !

Her Marriage.

'Twas morn—a most auspicious one !

From the Golden East, the Golden Sun

Came forth his glorious race to run,

   Through clouds of most splendid tinges ;

Clouds that lately slept in shade,

      But new seem'd made

      Of gold brocade,

With magnificent golden fringes.

Gold above, and gold below,

The earth reflected the golden glow,

   From river, and hill, and valley ;

Gilt by the golden light of morn,

The Thames—it look'd like the Golden Horn,

And the Barge, that carried coal or corn,

    Like Cleopatra's Galley !

Bright as clusters of Golden-rod,

Suburban poplars began to nod,

    With extempore splendour furnish'd ;

While London was bright with glittering clocks,

Golden dragons, and Golden cocks,

      And above them all,

      The dome of St. Paul,

With its Golden Cross and its Golden Ball,

    Shone out as if newly burnish'd !

And lo ! for Golden Hours and Joys,

Troops of glittering Golden Boys

Danced along with a jocund noise,

    And their gilded emblems carried !

In short, 'twas the year's most Golden Day,

By mortals call'd the First of May,

When Miss Kilmansegg,
Of the Golden Leg,
With a Golden Ring was married!

And thousands of children, women, and men,
Counted the clock from eight till ten,
From St. James's sonorous steeple;
For next to that interesting job,
The hanging of Jack, or Bill, or Bob,
There's nothing so draws a London mob
As the noosing of very rich people.

And a treat it was for a mob to behold
The Bridal Carriage that blazed with gold!
And the Footmen tall, and the Coachman bold,
In liveries so resplendent—
Coats you wonder'd to see in place,
They seem'd so rich with golden lace,
That they might have been independent.

Coats that made those menials proud
Gaze with scorn on the dingy crowd,

From their gilded elevations ;
Not to forget that saucy lad
(Ostentation's favourite cad),
The Page, who look'd, so splendidly clad,
  Like a Page of the " Wealth of Nations."

But the Coachman carried off the state,
With what was a Lancashire body of late
  Turn'd into a Dresden Figure ;
With a bridal Nosegay of early bloom,
About the size of a birchen broom,
And so huge a White Favour, had Gog been Groom
  He need not have worn a bigger.

And then to see the Groom ! the Count !
With Foreign Orders to such an amount.
  And whiskers so wild—nay, bestial ;
He seem'd to have borrow'd the shaggy hair
As well as the Stars of the Polar Bear,
  To make him look celestial !

And then—Great Jove !—the struggle, the crush,

The screams, the heaving, the awful rush,

   The swearing, the tearing, and fighting,

The hats and bonnets smash'd like an egg—

To catch a glimpse of the Golden Leg,

Which, between the steps and Miss Kilmansegg,

   Was fully display'd in alighting !

From the Golden Ankle up to the Knee

There it was for the mob to see !

A shocking act had it chanced to be

   A crooked leg or a skinny :

But although a magnificent veil she wore,

Such as never was seen before,

In case of blushes, she blush'd no more

   Than George the First on a guinea !

Another step, and lo ! she was launch'd !

All in white, as Brides are *blanch'd*,

   With a wreath of most wonderful splendour—

Diamonds, and pearls, so rich in device,

That, according to calculation nice,

Her head was worth as royal a price

    As the head of the Young Pretender.

Bravely she shone—and shone the more

As she sail'd through the crowd of squalid and poor,

    Thief, beggar, and tatterdemalion—

Led by the Count, with his sloe-black eyes

Bright with triumph, and some surprise,

Like Anson on making sure of his prize

    The famous Mexican Galleon!

Anon came Lady K., with her face

Quite made up to act with grace,

  . But she cut the performance shorter;

For instead of pacing stately and stiff,

At the stare of the vulgar she took a miff,

And ran, full speed, into Church, as if

    To get married before her daughter.

But Sir Jacob walk'd more slowly, and bow'd
Right and left to the gaping crowd,
   Wherever a glance was seizable ;
For Sir Jacob thought he bow'd like a Guelph,
And therefore bow'd to imp and elf,
And would gladly have made a bow to himself,
   Had such a bow been feasible.

And last—and not the least of the sight,
Six " Handsome Fortunes," all in white,
Came to help in the marriage rite,—
   And rehearse their own hymeneals ;
And then the bright procession to close,
They were followed by just as many Beaux
   Quite fine enough for Ideals.

Glittering men, and splendid dames,
Thus they enter'd the porch of St. James',
   Pursued by a thunder of laughter ;
For the Beadle was forced to intervene,

For Jim the Crow, and his Mayday Queen,

With her gilded ladle, and Jack i' the Green,

Would fain have follow'd after!

Beadle-like he hush'd the shout;

But the temple was full " inside and out,"

And a buzz kept buzzing all round about

　　Like bees when the day is sunny—

A buzz universal that interfered

With the rite that ought to have been revered,

As if the couple already were smear'd

　　With Wedlock's treacle and honey !

Yet Wedlock 's a very awful thing !

'Tis something like that feat in the ring

　　Which requires good nerve to do it—

When one of a " Grand Equestrian Troop "

Makes a jump at a gilded hoop,

　　　　Not certain at all

　　　　Of what may befall

After his getting through it !

But the Count he felt the nervous work
No more than any polygamous Turk,
  Or bold piratical schipper,
Who, during his buccaneering search,
Would as soon engage "a hand " in church
  As a hand on board his clipper!

And how did the Bride perform her part?
Like any Bride who is cold at heart,
  Mere snow with the ice's glitter;
What but a life of winter for her!
Bright but chilly, alive without stir,
So splendidly comfortless,—just like a Fir
  When the frost is severe and bitter.

Such were the future man and wife!
Whose bale or bliss to the end of life
  A few short words were to settle—
    Wilt thou have this woman ?
      I will—and then,
    Wilt thou have this man ?

I will, and Amen—

And those Two were one Flesh, in the Angels' ken,

Except one Leg—that was metal.

Then the names were sign'd—and kiss'd the kiss :

And the Bride, who came from her coach a Miss,

As a Countess walk'd to her carriage—

Whilst Hymen preen'd his plumes like a dove,

And Cupid flutter'd his wings above,

In the shape of a fly—as little a Love

As ever look'd in at a marriage !

Another crash—and away they dash'd,

And the gilded carriage and footmen flash'd

From the eyes of the gaping people—

Who turn'd to gaze at the toe-and-heel

Of the Golden Boys beginning a reel,

To the merry sound of a wedding-peal

From St. James's musical steeple.

Those wedding-bells ! those wedding-bells !

How sweetly they sound in pastoral dells

From a tow'r in an ivy-green jacket !

But town-made joys how dearly they cost ;

And after all are tumbled and tost,

Like a peal from a London steeple, and lost

In town-made riot and racket.

The wedding-peal, how sweetly it peals

With grass or heather beneath our heels,—

For bells are Music's laughter !—

But a London peal, well mingled, be sure,

With vulgar noises and voices impure,

What a harsh and discordant overture

To the Harmony meant to come after !

But hence with Discord—perchance, too soon

To cloud the face of the honeymoon

With a dismal occultation !—

Whatever Fate's concerted trick,

The Countess and Count, at the present nick,

Have a chicken and not a crow to pick

At a sumptuous Cold Collation.

A Breakfast—no unsubstantial mess,

But one in the style of Good Queen Bess,

Who,—hearty as hippocampus,—

Broke her fast with ale and beef,

Instead of toast and the Chinese leaf,

And in lieu of anchovy—grampus !

A breakfast of fowl, and fish, and flesh,

Whatever was sweet, or salt, or fresh ;

With wines the most rare and curious—

Wines, of the richest flavour and hue ;

With fruits from the worlds both Old and New ;

And fruits obtain'd before they were due

At a discount most usurious.

For wealthy palates there be, that scout

What is *in* season, for what is *out*,

And prefer all precocious savour :

For instance, early green peas, of the sort

That costs some four or five guineas a quart ;

Where the *Mint* is the principal flavour.

And many a wealthy man was there,

Such as the wealthy City could spare,

   To put in a portly appearance—

Men whom their fathers had help'd to gild :

And men who had had their fortunes to build

And—much to their credit—had richly fill'd

   Their purses by *pursy-verance.*

Men, by popular rumour at least,

Not the last to enjoy a feast!

   And truly they were not idle !

Luckier far than the chesnut tits,

Which, down at the door, stood champing their bitts,

   At a different sort of bridle.

For the time was come—and the whisker'd Count

Help'd his Bride in the carriage to mount,

   And fain would the Muse deny it,

But the crowd, including two butchers in blue,

(The regular killing Whitechapel hue,)

Of her Precious Calf had as ample a view,

   As if they had come to buy it !

Then away ! away ! with all the speed
That golden spurs can give to the steed,—
Both Yellow Boys and Guineas, indeed,
   Concurr'd to urge the cattle—
Away they went, with favours white,
Yellow jackets, and pannels bright,
And left the mob, like a mob at night,
   Agape at the sound of a rattle.

Away ! away ! they rattled and roll'd,
The Count, and his Bride, and her Leg of Gold—
   That faded charm to the charmer !
Away,—through Old Brentford rang the din,
Of wheels and heels, on their way to win
That hill, named after one of her kin,
   The Hill of the Golden Farmer !

Gold, still gold—it flew like dust !
It tipp'd the post-boy, and paid the trust ;
In each open palm it was freely thrust ;
   There was nothing but giving and taking !

And if gold could ensure the future hour,
What hopes attended that Bride to her bow'r,
But alas! even hearts with a four-horse pow'r
  Of opulence end in breaking!

Her Honeymoon.

The moon—the moon, so silver and cold,
Her fickle temper has oft been told,
  Now shady—now bright and sunny—
But of all the lunar things that change,
The one that shews most fickle and strange,
And takes the most eccentric range
  Is the moon—so called—of honey!

To some a full-grown orb reveal'd,
As big and as round as Norval's shield,
  And as bright as a burner Bude-lighted;
To others as dull, and dingy, and damp,
As any oleaginous lamp,
Of the regular old parochial stamp,
  In a London fog benighted.

To the loving, a bright and constant sphere,
That makes earth's commonest scenes appear
   All poetic, romantic, and tender :
Hanging with jewels a cabbage-stump,
And investing a common post, or a pump,
A currant-bush, or a gooseberry clump,
   With a halo of dreamlike splendour.

A sphere such as shone from Italian skies,
In Juliet's dear, dark, liquid eyes,
   Tipping trees with its argent braveries—
And to couples not favour'd with Fortune's boons,
One of the most delightful of moons,
For it brightens their pewter platters and spoons
   Like a silver service of Savory's !

For all is bright, and beauteous, and clear,
And the meanest thing most precious and dear,
   When the magic of love is present :
Love, that lends a sweetness and grace

To the humblest spot and the plainest face—
That turns Wilderness Row into Paradise Place,
  And Garlick Hill to Mount Pleasant !

Love that sweetens sugarless tea,
And makes contentment and joy agree
  With the coarsest boarding and bedding :
Love that no golden ties can attach,
But nestles under the humblest thatch,
And will fly away from an Emperor's match
  To dance at a Penny Wedding !

Oh, happy, happy, thrice happy state,
When such a bright Planet governs the fate
  Of a pair of united lovers !
'Tis theirs, in spite of the Serpent's hiss,
To enjoy the pure primeval kiss,
With as much of the old original bliss
  As mortality ever recovers !

There 's strength in double joints, no doubt,
In double X Ale, and Dublin Stout,

That the single sorts know nothing about—
   And a fist is strongest when doubled—
And double aqua-fortis, of course,
And double soda-water, perforce,
   Are the strongest that ever bubbled !

There 's double beauty whenever a Swan
Swims on a Lake, with her double thereon ;
And ask the gardener, Luke or John,
   Of the beauty of double-blowing—
A double dahlia delights the eye ;
And it 's far the loveliest sight in the sky
   When a double rainbow is glowing !

There 's warmth in a pair of double soles ;
As well as a double allowance of coals—
   In a coat that is double-breasted—
In double windows and double doors ;
And a double U wind is blest by scores
   For its warmth to the tender-chested.

There 's a twofold sweetness in double pipes ;
And a double barrel and double snipes
   Give the sportsman a duplicate pleasure :
There 's double safety in double locks ;
And double letters bring cash for the box ;
And all the world knows that double knocks
   Are gentility's double measure.

There 's a double sweetness in double rhymes,
And a double at Whist and a double Times
   In profit are certainly double—
By doubling, the Hare contrives to escape :
And all seamen delight in a doubled Cape,
   And a double-reef'd topsail in trouble.

There 's a double chuck at a double chin,
And of course there 's a double pleasure therein,
   If the parties were brought to telling :
And however our Dennises take offence,
A double meaning shews double sense ;

And if proverbs tell truth,

A double tooth

Is Wisdom's adopted dwelling !

But double wisdom, and pleasure, and sense,

Beauty, respect, strength, comfort, and thence

Through whatever the list discovers,

They are all in the double blessedness summ'd,

Of what was formerly double-drumm'd,

The Marriage of two true Lovers !

Now the Kilmansegg Moon—it must be told—

Though instead of silver it tipp'd with gold—

Shone rather wan, and distant, and cold,

And before its days were at thirty,

Such gloomy clouds began to collect,

With an ominous ring of ill effect,

As gave but too much cause to expect

Such weather as seamen call dirty !

And yet the moon was the " Young May Moon,"

And the scented hawthorn had blossom'd soon,

And the thrush and the blackbird were singing—
The snow-white lambs were skipping in play,
And the bee was humming a tune all day
To flowers as welcome as flowers in May,
    And the trout in the stream was springing !

But what were the hues of the blooming earth,
Its scents—its sounds—or the music and mirth
    Of its furr'd or its feather'd creatures,
To a Pair in the world's last sordid stage,
Who had never look'd into Nature's page,
And had strange ideas of a Golden Age,
    Without any Arcadian features ?

And what were joys of the pastoral kind
To a Bride—town-made—with a heart and mind
    With simplicity ever at battle ?
A bride of an ostentatious race,
Who, thrown in the Golden Farmer's place,
Would have trimm'd her shepherds with golden lace,
    And gilt the horns of her cattle.

She could not please the pigs with her whim,

And the sheep wouldn't cast their eyes at a limb

 For which she had been such a martyr :

The deer in the park, and the colts at grass.

And the cows unheeded let it pass ;

And the ass on the common was such an ass,

  That he wouldn't have swapp'd

  The thistle he cropp'd

 For her Leg, including the Garter !

She hated lanes, and she hated fields—

She hated all that the country yields—

 And barely knew turnips from clover :

She hated walking in any shape,

And a country stile was an awkward scrape,

Without the bribe of a mob to gape

 At the Leg in clambering over !

O blessed nature, " O rus ! O rus ! "

Who cannot sigh for the country thus,

 Absorbed in a worldly torpor—

Who does not yearn for its meadow-sweet breath,

Untainted by care, and crime, and death,

And to stand sometimes upon grass or heath—

    That soul, spite of gold, is a pauper !

But to hail the pearly advent of morn,

And relish the odour fresh from the thorn,

    She was far too pamper'd a madam—

Or to joy in the daylight waxing strong,

While, after ages of sorrow and wrong,

The scorn of the proud, the misrule of the strong,

And all the woes that to man belong,

The lark still carols the self-same song

    That he did to the uncurst Adam !

The Lark ! she had given all Leipsic's flocks

For a Vauxhall tune in a musical box ;

    And as for the birds in the thicket,

Thrush or ousel in leafy niche,

The linnet or finch, she was far too rich

To care for a Morning Concert to which

    She was welcome without any ticket.

Gold, still gold, her standard of old,

All pastoral joys were tried by gold,

  Or by fancies golden and crural—

Till ere she had pass'd one week unblest,

As her agricultural Uncle's guest,

Her mind was made up and fully imprest

  That felicity could not be rural!

And the Count?—to the snow-white lambs at play,

And all the scents and the sights of May,

  And the birds that warbled their passion,

His ears, and dark eyes, and decided nose,

Were as deaf and as blind and as dull as those

That overlook the Bouquet de Rose,

    The Huile Antique,

    And Parfum Unique,

  In a Barber's Temple of Fashion.

To tell, indeed, the true extent

Of his rural bias so far it went

  As to covet estates in ring fences—

And for rural lore he had learn'd in town
That the country was green, turn'd up with brown,
And garnish'd with trees that a man might cut down
    Instead of his own expenses.

And yet had that fault been his only one,
The Pair might have had few quarrels or none,
    For their tastes thus far were in common :
But faults he had that a haughty bride
With a Golden Leg could hardly abide—
Faults that would even have roused the pride
    Of a far less metalsome woman !

It was early days indeed for a wife,
In the very spring of her married life,
    To be chill'd by its wintry weather—
But instead of sitting as Love-Birds do,
Or Hymen's turtles that bill and coo—
Enjoying their " moon and honey for two "
    They were scarcely seen together !

In vain she sat with her Precious Leg
A little exposed, à la Kilmansegg,
　　And roll'd her eyes in their sockets !
He left her in spite of her tender regards,
And those loving murmurs described by bards,
For the rattling of dice and the shuffling of cards,
　　And the poking of balls into pockets !

Moreover he loved the deepest stake
And the heaviest bets the players would make ;
　　And he drank—the reverse of sparely,—
And he used strange curses that made her fret ;
And when he play'd with herself at piquet,
　　　　She found, to her cost,
　　　　For she always lost,
　　That the Count did not count quite fairly.

And then came dark mistrust and doubt,
Gather'd by worming his secrets out,
　　And slips in his conversations—
Fears, which all her peace destroy'd,

That his title was null— his coffers were void—
And his French Château was in Spain, or enjoy'd
   The most airy of situations.

But still his heart—if he had such a part—
She—only she—might possess his heart,
   And hold his affections in fetters—
Alas! that hope, like a crazy ship,
Was forced its anchor and cable to slip
When, seduced by her fears, she took a dip
   In his private papers and letters.

Letters that told of dangerous leagues ;
And notes that hinted as many intrigues
   As the Count's in the " Barber of Seville "—
In short such mysteries came to light,
That the Countess-Bride, on the thirtieth night,
Woke and started up in affright.
And kick'd and scream'd with all her might,
And finally fainted away outright,
   For she dreamt she had married the Devil!

Her Misery.

Who hath not met with home-made bread,
A heavy compound of putty and lead—
And home-made wines that rack the head,
 And home-made liqueurs and waters ?
Home-made pop that will not foam,
And home-made dishes that drive one from home,
  Not to name each mess,
  For the face or dress,
Home-made by the homely daughters ?

Home-made physic, that sickens the sick ;
Thick for thin and thin for thick ;—
In short each homogeneous trick
 For poisoning domesticity ?
And since our Parents, called the First,
A little family squabble nurst,
Of all our evils the worst of the worst
 Is home-made infelicity.

There 's a Golden Bird that claps its wings,
And dances for joy on its perch, and sings
   With a Persian exaltation :
For the Sun is shining into the room,
And brightens up the carpet-bloom,
As if it were new, bran new from the loom,
   Or the lone Nun's fabrication.

And thence the glorious radiance flames
On pictures in massy gilded frames—
Enshrining, however, no painted Dames,
   But portraits of colts and fillies—
Pictures hanging on walls which shine,
In spite of the bard's familiar line,
   With clusters of " gilded lilies."

And still the flooding sunlight shares
Its lustre with gilded sofas and chairs,
   That shine as if freshly burnish'd—
And gilded tables, with glittering stocks

Of gilded china, and golden clocks,
Toy, and trinket, and musical box,
   That Peace and Paris have furnish'd.

And lo! with the brightest gleam of all
The glowing sunbeam is seen to fall
   On an object as rare as splendid—
The golden foot of the Golden Leg
Of the Countess—once Miss Kilmansegg—
   But there all sunshine is ended.

Her cheek is pale, and her eye is dim,
And downward cast, yet not at the limb,
   Once the centre of all speculation ;
But downward drooping in comfort's dearth,
As gloomy thoughts are drawn to the earth—
Whence human sorrows derive their birth—
   By a moral gravitation.

Her golden hair is out of its braids,
And her sighs betray the gloomy shades
   That her evil planet revolves in—

And tears are falling that catch a gleam
So bright as they drop in the sunny beam,
That tears of *aqua regia* they seem,
   The water that gold dissolves in !

Yet, not in filial grief were shed
   Those tears for a mother's insanity ;
Nor yet because her father was dead,
For the bowing Sir Jacob had bow'd his head
   To Death—with his usual urbanity ;
The waters that down her visage rill'd
Were drops of unrectified spirit distill'd
   From the limbeck of Pride and Vanity.

Tears that fell alone and uncheckt,
Without relief, and without respect,
Like the fabled pearls that the pigs neglect,
   When pigs have that opportunity—
And of all the griefs that mortals share,
The one that seems the hardest to bear
   Is the grief without community.

How bless'd the heart that has a friend
A sympathising ear to lend
    To troubles too great to smother !
For as ale and porter, when flat, are restored
Till a sparkling bubbling head they afford,
So sorrow is cheer'd by being pour'd
    From one vessel into another.

But friend or gossip she had not one
To hear the vile deeds that the Count had done,
    How night after night he rambled :
And how she had learn'd by sad degrees
That he drank, and smoked, and worse than these,
    That he " swindled, intrigued, and gambled."

How he kiss'd the maids, and sparr'd with John ;
And came to bed with his garments on ;
    With other offences as heinous—
And brought *strange* gentlemen home to dine,
That he said were in the Fancy Line,
And they fancied spirits instead of wine,
    And call'd her lap-dog " Wenus."

Of " making a book " how he made a stir,
But never had written a line to her,
　　Once his idol and Cara Sposa :
And how he had storm'd, and treated her ill,
Because she refused to go down to a mill,
She didn't know where, but remember'd still
　　That the Miller's name was Mendoza.

How often he waked her up at night,
And oftener still by the morning light,
　　Reeling home from his haunts unlawful ;
Singing songs that shouldn't be sung,
Except by beggars and thieves unhung—
Or volleying oaths, that a foreign tongue
　　Made still more horrid and awful !

How oft, instead of otto of rose,
With vulgar smells he offended her nose,
　　From gin, tobacco, and onion !
And then how wildly he used to stare !
And shake his fist at nothing, and swear,-

And pluck by the handful his shaggy hair,

Till he look'd like a study of Giant Despair

   For a new Edition of Bunyan !

           ♥

For dice will run the contrary way,

As well is known to all who play,

   And cards will conspire as in treason :

And what with keeping a hunting-box,

      Following fox—

      Friends in flocks,

      Burgundies, Hocks,

      From London Docks ;

      Stultz's frocks,

      Manton and Nock's

      Barrels and locks,

      Shooting blue rocks,

      Trainers and jocks,

      Buskins and socks,

      Pugilistical knocks,

      And fighting-cocks,

If he found himself short in funds and stocks,

   These rhymes will furnish the reason!

His friends, indeed, were falling away—
Friends who insist on play or pay—
And he fear'd at no very distant day
    To be cut by Lord and by cadger,
As one who was gone or going to smash,
For his cheeks no longer drew the cash,
Because, as his comrades explain'd in flash.
    " He had overdrawn his badger."

Gold, gold—alas ! for the gold
Spent where souls are bought and sold,
    In Vice's Walpurgis revel !
Alas ! for muffles, and bulldogs, and guns.
The leg that walks, and the leg that runs,
All real evils, though Fancy ones.
When they lead to debt, dishonour, and duns.
    Nay, to death, and perchance the devil !

Alas ! for the last of a Golden race !
Had she cried her wrongs in the market-place.
    She had warrant for all her clamour—
For the worst of rogues, and brutes, and rakes,

Was breaking her heart by constant aches,

With as little remorse as the Pauper who breaks

A flint with a parish hammer !

Her Last Will.

Now the Precious Leg while cash was flush,

Or the Count's acceptance worth a rush,

Had never excited dissension ;

But no sooner the stocks began to fall,

Than, without any ossification at all,

The limb became what people call

A perfect bone of contention.

For alter'd days brought alter'd ways,

And instead of the complimentary phrase,

So current before her bridal—

The Countess heard, in language low,

That her Precious Leg was precious slow,

A good 'un to look at but bad to go,

And kept quite a sum lying idle.

That instead of playing musical airs,
Like Colin's foot in going up-stairs—
As the wife in the Scottish ballad declares—
   It made an infernal stumping.
Whereas a member of cork, or wood,
Would be lighter and cheaper and quite as good,
   Without the unbearable thumping.

P'rhaps she thought it a decent thing
To shew her calf to cobbler and king,
   But nothing could be absurder—
While none but the crazy would advertise
Their gold before their servants' eyes,
Who of course some night would make it a prize,
   By a Shocking and Barbarous Murder.

But spite of hint, and threat, and scoff,
   The Leg kept its situation :
For legs are not to be taken off
   By a verbal amputation.
And mortals when they take a whim,
The greater the folly the stiffer the limb

That stands upon it or by it—
So the Countess, then Miss Kilmansegg,
At her marriage refused to stir a peg,
Till the Lawyers had fastened on her Leg,
  As fast as the Law could tie it.

Firmly then—and more firmly yet—
With scorn for scorn, and with threat for threat,
  The Proud One confronted the Cruel :
And loud and bitter the quarrel arose,
Fierce and merciless—one of those,
With spoken daggers, and looks like blows,
  In all but the bloodshed a duel !

Rash, and wild, and wretched, and wrong,
Were the words that came from Weak and Strong,
  Till madden'd for desperate matters,
Fierce as tigress escaped from her den,
She flew to her desk—'twas open'd—and then,
In the time it takes to try a pen,
Or the clerk to utter his slow Amen,
  Her Will was in fifty tatters !

But the Count, instead of curses wild,
Only nodded his head and smiled,
As if at the spleen of an angry child ;
    But the calm was deceitful and sinister !
A lull like the lull of the treacherous sea—
For Hate in that moment had sworn to be
The Golden Leg's sole Legatee,
    And that very night to administer !

Her Death.

'Tis a stern and startling thing to think
How often mortality stands on the brink
    Of its grave without any misgiving :
And yet in this slippery world of strife,
In the stir of human bustle so rife,
There are daily sounds to tell us that Life
    Is dying, and Death is living !

Ay, Beauty the Girl, and Love the Boy,
Bright as they are with hope and joy,
    How their souls would sadden instanter.

To remember that one of those wedding bells,

Which ring so merrily through the dells,

Is the same that knells

Our last farewells,

Only broken into a canter !

But breath and blood set doom at nought—

How little the wretched Countess thought,

When at night she unloosed her sandal,

That the Fates had woven her burial-cloth,

And that Death, in the shape of a Death's Head Moth,

Was fluttering round her candle !

As she look'd at her clock of or-molu,

For the hours she had gone so wearily through

At the end of a day of trial—

How little she saw in her pride of prime

The dart of Death in the Hand of Time—

That hand which moved on the dial !

As she went with her taper up the stair,

How little her swollen eye was aware

That the Shadow which follow'd was double !
Or when she closed her chamber door,
It was shutting out, and for evermore,
  The world—and its worldly trouble.

Little she dreamt, as she laid aside
Her jewels—after one glance of pride—
  They were solemn bequests to Vanity—
Or when her robes she began to doff,
That she stood so near to the putting off
  Of the flesh that clothes humanity.

And when she quench'd the taper's light,
How little she thought as the smoke took flight,
That her day was done—and merged in a night
  Of dreams and duration uncertain—
      Or, along with her own,
      That a Hand of Bone
  Was closing mortality's curtain !

But life is sweet, and mortality blind,
And youth is hopeful, and Fate is kind

In concealing the day of sorrow ;   .
And enough is the present tense of toil—
For this world is, to all, a stiffish soil—
And the mind flies back with a glad recoil
　From the debts not due till to-morrow.

Wherefore else does the Spirit fly
And bid its daily cares good-bye,
　Along with its daily clothing ?
Just as the felon condemned to die—
　With a very natural loathing—
Leaving the Sheriff to dream of ropes,
From his gloomy cell in a vision elopes,
To caper on sunny greens and slopes,
　Instead of the dance upon nothing.

Thus, even thus, the Countess slept,
While Death still nearer and nearer crept,
　Like the Thane who smote the sleeping—
But her mind was busy with early joys,
Her golden treasures and golden toys,

That flash'd a bright
And golden light
Under lids still red with weeping.

The golden doll that she used to hug !
Her coral of gold, and the golden mug !
Her godfather's golden presents !
The golden service she had at her meals,
The golden watch, and chain, and seals,
Her golden scissors, and thread, and reels,
And her golden fishes and pheasants !

The golden guineas in silken purse—
And the Golden Legends she heard from her nurse,
Of the Mayor in his gilded carriage—
And London streets that were paved with gold—
And the Golden Eggs that were laid of old—
With each golden thing
To the golden ring
At her own auriferous Marriage !

And still the golden light of the sun
Through her golden dream appear'd to run,
Though the night that roar'd without was one
   To terrify seamen or gipsies—
While the moon, as if in malicious mirth,
Kept peeping down at the ruffled earth,
As though she enjoyed the tempest's birth,
   In revenge of her old eclipses.

But vainly, vainly, the thunder fell,
For the soul of the Sleeper was under a spell
   That time had lately embitter'd—
The Count, as once at her foot he knelt—
That foot which now he wanted to melt !
But—hush!—'twas a stir at her pillow she felt—
   And some object before her glitter'd.

'Twas the Golden Leg !—she knew its gleam !
And up she started, and tried to scream,—
   But ev'n in the moment she started—

Down came the limb with a frightful smash,
And, lost in the universal flash
That her eyeballs made at so mortal a crash,
   The Spark, called Vital, departed!

          *   *   *   *   *

Gold, still gold! hard, yellow, and cold,
For gold she had lived, and she died for gold—
   By a golden weapon—not oaken ;
In the morning they found her all alone—
Stiff, and bloody, and cold as stone—
But her Leg, the Golden Leg, was gone,
   And the " Golden Bowl was broken ! "

Gold—still gold ! it haunted her yet—
At the Golden Lion the Inquest met—
   Its foreman, a carver and gilder—
And the Jury debated from twelve till three
What the Verdict ought to be,
And they brought it in as Felo de Se,
   " Because her own Leg had killed her ! "

Her Moral.

Gold! Gold! Gold! Gold!
Bright and yellow, hard and cold,
Molten, graven, hammer'd, and roll'd ;
Heavy to get, and light to hold ;
Hoarded, barter'd, bought, and sold,
Stolen, borrow'd, squander'd, doled :
Spurn'd by the young, but hugg'd by the old
To the very verge of the churchyard mould ;
Price of many a crime untold ;
Gold! Gold! Gold! Gold:
Good or bad a thousand-fold !

How widely its agencies vary—
To save—to ruin—to curse—to bless—
As even its minted coins express,
Now stamped with the image of Good Queen Bess,
And now of a Bloody Mary !

END OF VOL. I.

BRADBURY AND EVANS, PRINTERS, WHITEFRIARS.